T0275018

The Tears

SEAGULL
BOOKS
·
CELEBRATING
40 YEARS

THE FRENCH LIST

CONTENTS

I

(The Book of the Heidelbeermann)

II

(The Book of the Inscrutable Heart)

III

(Wo Europa anfängt?)

IV

(The Book of Angilbert's Poem)

V

(The Book about the Sixteenth of the Kalends of March)

VI

(The Book of the Death of Nithard)

VII

(The Sequence of Saint Eulalia)

VIII

(The Book of Eden)

IX

(The Book of the Poet Virgil)

X

(*Liber eruditorum*)

I

(The Book of the Heidelbeermann)

1. Story of Horses

Once upon a time, horses ran free. They galloped on the Earth without men desiring them, encircling them, rounding them up in gorges, lassoing them, trapping them, hitching them to chariots, harnessing them, saddling them, shoeing them, mounting them, sacrificing them, eating them. Sometimes men and animals sang together. The long moans of the one group led to the strange whinnying of the other. The birds came down from the sky to peck at the crumbs to be found between the legs of the horses, which shook their magnificent manes, and between the thighs of the men who threw back their heads as, seated on the floor around the fire, they ate hungrily, noisily, excessively and suddenly clapped their hands in time. When the fire had gone out, when they had finished singing, the men got up again. For the men did not sleep standing as the horses did. Then they wiped from the floor the traces from their scrotum and genitals that had been left there. They got back on their horses and rode over the whole face of the Earth, over the damp seashores, through the low, primal forests, over the windy heathlands, the steppes. One day, a young man made up this song: 'I came out of a woman and found myself facing death. Where does my spirit stray to at night? In what world does it reside? And so, there is a face I've never seen that pursues me. Why do I keep seeing this face I do not know?'

He set off alone on horseback.

Suddenly, as he was galloping in full daylight, night fell.

He leaned over. Fearful, he stroked the hair on the neck of his mount and its warm, trembling skin.

But the sky turned utterly black.

The horseman tugged on the little bronze chain of the reins. He dismounted. He unfurled on the ground a blanket made from three reindeer pelts securely knotted together. He tied its four corners together, so as to protect both himself and his horse's face as completely as possible. They set off again.

The air was still.

Suddenly, rain hammered down on them.

They moved along slowly, trying to make out their path amid the din and the booming rain. They came to a hilltop. It had stopped raining. There were three men tied to branches in the darkness.

In the middle, a stark-naked man with a crown of thorns on his brow was screaming.

Mysteriously, another man held a sponge to his lips on the end of a reed. By his sides at the same time a soldier was driving his spear into his heart.

2. Story that Happened to Hagus

One day later, centuries later, as night was falling, as, alone and on foot, he was leading his horse by the bridle along the banks of the Somme, in the half-darkness that was beginning to come over the river, he stopped.

The man had spotted a dead jay on a pile of slates.

This was some ten yards from the silently flowing river.

An alder tree stood there.

On the pile of loose greyish slates exposed to the light of the setting sun, a jay lay on its back, wings wide apart, beak open.

The horse snorted. But the man stroked the long heavy hair that ran down its spine.

Hagus, who was the ferryman, tied his boat to the trunk of the big alder tree. He came and stood beside the puzzled horseman and the motionless horse. With his ferryman's pole over his shoulder, he looked where they were looking.

There was, as it happened, something strange about this dead jay.

Then Hagus took his courage in both hands and went over to the blue-winged bird.

But he stopped almost immediately, for the jay was raising its black and sky-blue feathers in an even motion. It turned a little as it breathed. It was going about all this as follows: lifting a wing first towards the riverbank and the boat and the leaves of the alder and the river; then towards the thistles, the anxious motionless horse and the horseman paralysed by what he was seeing.

The jay was, in fact, offering up its colourful feathers to the last heat of the sun.

It was drying them.

Then, in under a second, it spun round, got back to its feet and, in a single bound, flew up on to the end of the ferryman's pole.

Then Hagus felt, upon his shoulder, that it was time to leave this world.

He turned his head towards the watching bird, which screeched horribly, then towards the horseman, but there was nothing there beside him now. The horseman and the horse had gone, though he had not seen them go.

Suddenly the bird unfurled its wings again, black and blue, left its perch—which was Hagus' pole resting on his shoulder—and flew away.

It vanished into the sky.

Hagus' character grew gradually gloomier. He began by neglecting his work on the river. He abandoned his boat in the reeds. He allowed the showers to fill it with rainwater. By the time two more seasons had passed, his wife and son were weary of his sadness. After some frenzied conversation, they gathered up their things and left. Then Hagus, having renounced the company of his family, turned away also from his friends. Or, rather, he stopped speaking to human beings. He avoided bright light. All that was visible frightened him. He even shunned the faces of animals, which to him seemed reproachful. He made detours to avoid meeting the gaze of a yellow-beaked buzzard or a frog which, in the warm night, was trying to attract him out on to the heathland with its song.

3. The Concert Box

There was once a slightly lame man who carried a partitioned box on his back. He went from hamlet to hamlet. He would put the box down on a stone or tree trunk or chest or bench and carefully open the lid. There were twelve compartments in it. Each contained a frog. In the evening, he looked up to the sky and called on Van Sissou. It was like a prayer raised to the heavens by the man with the crippled foot. 'Speak, Van Sissou!' he would exclaim, and he would ask one of the children present to take a jug and pour some water onto each head. The frogs sang.

'If you were quiet,' he would tell the children and the various groups of people who came in from the fields and forest paths, who gathered around and crowded in on him to examine the inside of his box, 'you would hear a muffled peal of chimes.'

Then even the children fell silent and listened to the song that gradually rose from the box and their eyes grew moist because all of them had known someone in the other world. Some muttered, 'Mummy' and their knees gave way beneath them. And they murmured, 'Mummy! Mummy!'

4. Nithard's Birth

Long ago, the day Nithard was born, Count Angilbert— who was the father of the child and also the abbot of the abbey dedicated to Saint Richarius in the Bay of the Somme—took the child as he emerged streaming with blood from Bertha's womb and said, 'You eyelids that lift for the very first time, creasing your fragile skin as you bare your two big wet eyes in the light, I bless you in the name of the father, the son and the holy spirit.' At that point, a new cry was heard. There was a twin in Bertha's belly: you could see the yellow forehead pushing against the wall of the womb and showing already between Bertha's great purplish-blue lips, just below the bush of blonde hair that covered her burstingly taut skin right up to the navel. The Count-Abbot Angilbert tried to grasp him. But the baby was particularly wet. The little slimy body writhed in all directions and slipped like an eel from his hands. The abbot cried out: 'You senses that begin to seek for purchase everywhere in nature, you tiny fingers that open and cling with such tenacity and ardour to the large hand of the one who conceived you some seasons past, I bless you in your turn. It is a sign God is sending to us by repeating the birth of Nithard with this face that resembles him even more than a shadow: it is almost a mirror image! God has wished to give him a companion for his days in the same way as he himself had John sleeping on his shoulder!'

Having uttered these words, he moved on to the second baptism and named the child Hartnid.

5. Nithard's Conception

Long ago, nine months before Nithard was born, one afternoon when they were hidden from view behind the yellow and white honeysuckle and the big blue wisteria, the emperor's daughter, whose name was Berehta or Bertha, took Count Angilbert's hand and said, 'Enter me.'

She repeated, 'Enter me. I love you so much.'

She lifted her tunic. Then he entered her.

She climaxed.

He enjoyed it so much himself that he penetrated her a second time.

She climaxed.

This happened before the birth of Nithard and Hartnid. At that time, Sar, the shaman of the Bay of the Somme, improvised this poem:

For, if birds love to sing, they also love to hear singing.

They love to hear the North Sea whose waves break beneath the chalk cliffs and they gradually fall silent as the waves rise and crash against the sand which they roll flat, the sand which they make by gnawing away at the vertical white wall.

The mere quivering of the reeds above the stagnant waters of the pools beside the bay attracts them.

The birds come to the salt meadows and the reed beds. They fly into the reeds. They like to accompany the songs the wind makes in the reed beds with their own trilling sounds.

Having said that—says Sar—the rain,

when it falls on the forest leaves,

cows them, by contrast, into silence.

It slows the rate of their variations and lowers the pitch of the sounds they warble.

Sometimes the downpours and showers put a stop to them.

Their chirpings give way entirely to the din and roar.

All birds respond. Even their surprising silence, when they happen to fall silent, is a response.

All birds modulate, depending on how place offers an accompaniment to the movements and particular resonance laid down for them by the strange mandates they obey.

Scarcely a single arpeggio rings out when it is foggy.

No string of calls is heard twice from birds in cover.

Bass notes travel further than treble in the world of birds—like pain in our own.

Slow notes are more easily distinguishable than fast.

I, Sar, say:

The signs of the birds are gentler than the sadness you feel.

They are more comprehensible to my ear than the language uttered by the people I assist when they are possessed—people in pain who, even as they suffer, don't know what to do with their suffering.

6. Hartnid in Love

One day, Matthew the Evangelist wrote in his Gospel 13:1—*In illo die, Iesu, exiens de domo, sedebat secus mare.* (One day, Jesus went out of his house and sat down by the sea.) One day, Hartnid went out of his house and sat down by the sea. The wind suddenly rose and whipped up the sand. He was thirteen. There was a boat there. He boarded the boat. He hoisted the sail on the mast. He sailed towards the west, then turned north and let go of the tiller. He fell asleep. Then he sailed for a long time. He crossed the sea and made land at Arklow. In Arklow Bay, Hartnid met a saint who lived under a rock.

Hartnid drew a face in the sand and asked the saint: 'Do you know this face?'

But the hermit replied, 'I don't know that face. Why do you ask me this question? I didn't even know you or your body or your face when I saw you just now, from the door of my stone cottage, anchoring your vessel, putting your little boat into the water with a rope, rowing it ashore and pulling it onto the briny mud and the fragments of broken shells.

'Because I am looking for the woman who has this face on her shoulders. That is the reason for my voyage. *My* face doesn't count. For my face existed already in this world when I appeared in this world.'

In the year 813, princess Beretha (Bertha, who was Hartnid's mother), said in her father's new palace at Aix-la-Chapelle:

'I think his head has emptied. Since the moment hair grew along his legs and reached his cheeks, love has changed him completely. Another body than his own has got into his brain, though I don't know where he got the vision of that body from. I know at least that, when he was twelve or thirteen, an image hoisted itself into his head and took hold of him. When the dawn came and he rose from his bed, that image didn't fade. From that moment on, he didn't want to see his brother. That image has become such an obsession that he hears nothing of what you say to him. He wants to find that face again. No one can be with my son without being stupefied by what he has become. He loves someone.'

This is how Princess Bertha justified her son's departure to the younger of her twins who was called Nithard. For, with twins, the first to be conceived is the last one out. This is how Hartnid—which was another way of writing Nithard—who had been conceived and named by Angilbert and carried in her womb and nourished by Bertha, left coastal Francia.

7. Frater Lucius

One of the monks at the Monastery of Saint-Riquier—of Saint Richarius—the one who taught Nithard and Hartnid their letters, both Greek and Latin, who was an excellent copyist and the most skilled scribe in the monastery at decorating the Byzantine letters and simplifying the Carolingian ones in the purest of ways, was named Frater Lucius. He had fallen in love with a cat that was entirely black. The cat was as handsome and slender as a little crow from the woods. It had gorgeous eyes. It was in fact more like a ploughland rook, as it had a white spot on its mouth. Brother Lucius looked forward to his day being ended, to his copy being finished and to leaving the scriptorium, even though the booths were heated with little footwarmers filled with embers, the heat from which built up beneath the monks' habits. But heat mattered little to him: Frater Lucius was bent on getting back to his cell and opening the wooden panel in its window, so that the cat could appear, jump in and plunge its freezing nose into the crook of his neck. He had thoughts only for his cat. He dreamt only of its caresses, caresses that were so hungry for caresses themselves, and of its subdued murmurings, gentle snorings, muffled cries, purring, lisping and little raspy licks, its eyes that blinked in acquiescence and half closed themselves in gentle repose.

Frater Lucius could think only of its tender little gaze and its heartbreaking little nose.

As soon as he had closed the door of his cell behind him, he removed his cowl. Once the hood was off, he pulled the wooden panel towards him and the cat was already leaping on to his shoulder and touching his cheek with its paw as though to caress it.

He didn't even need to whisper its name in the darkness across the monastery roofs. The cat jumped onto his shoulder and was already purring.

The two of them lay down on the palliasse of barley straw covered with animal pelts and fell asleep together.

The monk sank his face into the cat's fur. It was difficult to breathe like that but it seemed to revive him. They talked together. They were happy. They loved each other.

8. The Abbey Angilbert Restored

When the emperor offered Saint Marcoul's spring, the chapiteau of dry stone construction that overtopped it, the old hermitage of Saint Richarius the shaman king that had been built alongside it, and lastly the more recent buildings of the abbey that surrounded them to the count and abbot (*abbas et comes*) Angilbert, he gifted him all the outlying buildings as far as the seashore down below Quentovic. This was in the 790s. Harun-al-Rashid was already Caliph of the great city of Baghdad. Charlemagne was not yet emperor. No one in the world called him Carolus Magnus at this point, nor Charles le Magne, nor Karel der Grosse. The young king of the Franks did not want the count who ruled over the duchy of coastal Francia for a son-in-law. He was keen to bring Bertha back to his court right away. He loved Bertha more than any of the other princesses and even more than his wives. Here is what Count Angilbert found to say to Princess Bertha when, conforming with the request that her father had made to him, he rejected her forever:

'It may be that women and men do not know desire twice. I am not convinced of this, either in the case of men or women, but it is something that is possible. The fish we call salmon die just at the moment when they experience climax, even though it is the first time in their lives they have encountered it. From the moment their bodies and fins intermingle with the mountain springs where they were conceived, their old bodies, sodden with seed, and still shuddering from sexual delight, die. You noticed that something comparable happened to me in the honeysuckle, when we were in the shade of the heavy clusters of blue wisteria that hid us from the eyes of the other members of the court. Our bodies trembled in happiness exactly as animals do when they are afraid. One cries out at the last moment sometimes, when the soul escapes, as one cries when one is born, when the body discovers the light of the sun. And it happens that one cries out in pleasure, when the water one contains suddenly pours out. It is possible, indeed, that one doesn't learn very much by living. For the moment, your father has expressed the wish that we should touch each other no more. So far as I am concerned, that ruler is a friend and I a loyal companion. As for you, he is your father and you are a cheerful, loving daughter. He has had enough of his sons, and of the sons of his sons, and he fears for the succession of the vast kingdom he is eager to expand. You are going to go back to the palatine court of his women at Aix-la-Chappelle. Our bodies will not tremble again with either bliss or fear. I shall take care of our sons, and the three hundred monks I have gathered together at my abbey will instruct them as attentively as—and even more diligently than—all the other dukes on earth. The women who work at the ovens, who wash and dry the linen and who till the soil, plant and harvest in the rectangular abbey close will cherish them.'

Princess Bertha replied to Count Angilbert, who had become Father Abbot of the Abbey of Saint-Riquier:

'We women do not lead happy lives. The time when we are women is too short. We are girls for much too long and remain women for so few seasons. We are mothers too quickly and lose an interminable amount of time being old, heavily powdered women lingering on, hesitating to sink into the ocean of death. Moreover, the cycle of our fertility is disagreeably limited, if we compare it to the length of our existence. The care required by the little ones who emerge from our wombs is repetitive and sordid. This is why I think that our time as mothers and grandmothers is much too drawn out, to the point where it becomes wearisome and almost disgusting. In that sense, I am not at all unhappy to return to the company of my father at the age I am. My friend, continue to grant me your aid, since you no longer wish to lie beside my flesh, since you no longer wish to bring your mouth to my breast and suckle a little at the dry teat when evening has come, since you no longer wish to make your low moan in the crook of my shoulder. But now I am going to tell you what I think is the worst. The most dreadful thing in the existence women lead is that we love men whereas they desire us. Each of us women gives our self entirely to one of them, while as soon as they have pen-etrated us, they forget they are in our arms and run around seeking everywhere to learn what they never know.'

9. The Bath Scene in the Great Hall

Hartnid took his bath in his wooden tub in the great hall that was largely in darkness. He heard a woman's voice behind his back.

'Close your eyes when I touch you!'

Hartnid closed his eyes and answered the voice:

'I did as you asked. I have my two eyelids lowered. Do what you are readying yourself to do.'

Then the woman, called Wicklow, grabbed him by the shoulders and got into the tub.

He opened his eyes. He looked at her. She was very beautiful. He told her: 'I shan't have to close my eyes any more when you come to me.'

'Alas.'

'You will be my only wife. You are so beautiful. You are the first woman I have seen naked. Even the woman whose face I seek, I cannot imagine her nudity. You will be the only one whose full, immodest appearance I shall know and I shall place it by the portrait that long ago fixed itself— I know not why—in my heart.'

The woman looked sad.

She said: 'There will only be dreams now to bring life their aid.'

Then the woman pointed to the edge of the tub. 'What is that bird on the copper rim?'

'That is my jay.'

10. The Defeat of Abdul Rahman al-Ghafiqi

What do we call horror? A sense of dread which fear suddenly produces throughout the body, from top to toe. It makes the hairs bristle or the fur stand on end. Nothing prepares you for it. It even robs you of your sleep. Or it strikes to interrupt sleep and is like a wrenching that seizes it, that grips it by the throat like a snare, covers the belly with sweat, drenches the furrow between the buttocks. In the state of horror, no tears flow. In most wild animals, all of them endowed with extraordinary prescience, it produces an irresistible desire for headlong flight. At the same moment, two attacks combined and strangled Europe like fangs. A progressive, learned, pious, subtle invasion in the south; a brutal, barbaric, greedy, violent invasion in the north. Between them, the one, which became a running sore, marked by wonderful singing to the accompaniment of vielle music, and the other, sporadic and burning everything in its path, held the continent in a vice-like grip, without any pre-concerted plan on the part of either. In 698, only Carthage, which happened to be the finest port then dominating the Mediterranean, had fallen into Arab hands. By 711, the entire sea had been conquered. Over the whole periphery of the inner sea, Saracen towers were built along the coasts, which bristled with them like so many spears. The Byzantine Eastern Empire, now shrunken to the area around the Sea of Marmora, no longer had any direct contact with the Western part of the old empire. The ports of Provence emptied. Fishing smacks, open boats and barges replaced the ships, reduced in size, the galleys, shortened in length, and the long merchants' péniches, which were miniaturized to the point where they became tow-boats or even gondolas. The silks and spices from the Far East now crossed Italy's roads on the backs of donkeys. They snaked around the Alpine passes. They had difficulty getting through from India, from the plateaus of Mongolia, from the peaks of the Himalayas and from China's vast rivers.

Once the sea had fallen entirely into their hands, the Arabs moved on to the interiors.

After they had become masters of the Rhone valley, they subjugated Burgundy. They invested the city of Autun in 725. In 731, they besieged the old city of Sens, whence they were repulsed in the end by the archbishop, who had taken refuge on his island and attacked them from behind from the Jewish ghetto adjacent to the port, on the eastern arm of the navigable river. In 732 Charles Martel managed to meet up with Odo, Duke of Aquitaine and they combined their forces.

It was at that point that Abdul Rahman al-Ghafiqi lost the great battle fought at the gates of Poitiers.

In 733, Spanish Arab troops lost Lyon.

Only the Marseille aristocracy, which had allied with the Saracens against the Franks, remained staunchly Mohammedan.

11. The Council of Verneuil-sur-Avre

Suddenly, one day in 755 at Verneuil-sur-Avre, Pepin, King of the Franks, decided to postpone war from March to May.

A council was called and transformed warfare on European territory for a thousand years.

Among the ancient Romans, the double doors of war opened in March and closed again amid the downpours, mud and dead leaves of autumn. In the language spoken by the ancient warriors of Etruria, these doors were called *janua*.

Januarius deus patuleius et clusius. (January god of the door that opens and closes.)

The doors of January bore the enigmatic double face of an old man (*senex*) turned towards the West and a young child (*puer*) turned towards the East, sitting atop the stone of the *bifrons* year, while the previous year's king, with his long white hair, was being put to death—hanging from the branch of an oak, his skin being flayed from him.

Suddenly, marvellously, the new year was born with the first flowers.

The 'ia' in the Roman word *iannus* meant that which goes—the army being raised, the horses setting out, the clashing of weapons in the first light of the year.

So it was that in 755 the bishops gathered at Pepin's court in the old city built on the banks of the Iton and encircled by the Avre. They decreed that in this case, as they fell in willingly behind the view of the sovereign among the leaders (dukes) of the Frankish tribes, there would henceforth be two assemblies (*concilia*) each 'year' within the immense expanse where the Frankish horsemen rode. The one would be in May in the presence of the king and his troops of warriors for the review of the troops and the *placitum generalis*. The other would be in October and would be devoted to the administration of the kingdom, in the presence of the king's household, the leaders commanding the Frankish tribes, the abbots who ruled over the religious houses and the bishops who governed the dioceses.

In this way, the solidarity of the *vassi* would be concentrated around the person of the king in spring. In the autumn, the *missi* would be scattered abroad. And so the great ecclesiastical districts would be inspected one by one and the taxes raised annually. It was in this way that vassalage within each province and missions across the territory of the empire were balanced out. But, increasingly, the passes, river banks, shorelines and marches of the empire were breached, penetrated, pillaged, set ablaze, ransomed. The Arabs' forays gave way to the terrible, unpredictable raids of the Norsemen, amplifying the devastation on all sides, on all rivers and seas, on all borders, and even into the mountains.

12. What Was Called the Day of the Bear

One day long ago, a little village perched up in the Haut-Vallespir organized what they called a Dia de l'Ós. This was a rite that took place, between the peaks and passes of the steep mountains of the Pyrenees, as winter drew to a close. At the time, *Jour de l'Ours* [Day of the Bear] was the name given to a topsy-turvy festival that went back to the first men who had lived there long before the Basques, coming from Siberia, chased them out and attempted to annihilate them. These ancient peoples loved to get high on the juice of mushrooms. They would take torches and go into the caves, painting the cave walls using the embers from their fires. After stripping stark naked, the young men of the village blacked up their skin and the hair on their heads and body, using soot which they had mixed beforehand with fat. They put on the hides they had cut from sheep, after first turning them inside out and bloodying them. Armed with long sticks, the 'bears' tried to come down from the mountain heights towards the peasant holdings, the sheepfolds, the springs, the byres and the hamlets, while 'hunters' sought to repel them. The bears captured girls, whom they daubed with their blood and soot, attempting to carry them off against their will to the caves where they raped them and made them pregnant. Once the 'bears' had been satisfied and fallen asleep, the 'barbers', dressed in white and with painted faces, entered the caves where the wild beasts had committed their 'carnage' and captured them. They put them in chains and, with their wrists and ankles shackled, took them down to the village. Then, using a flint double axe, they shaved them completely, removing the hair from their head, arms, chests and armpits and from around the scrotum and penis. Then the women threw buckets of water over them and the beasts became men again. That day, Lucia was conceived by Ansiera, who was raped by the Count of Vannes and Prefect of Brittany, a man by the name of Hruodlandus (Roland) in the month of May of the year 777, as they were crossing the mountain passes. Later, Lucia had a daughter and the child had such blue eyes that she was named Lucilla.

13. The Origin of the Somme

The first colour that forms on the retina of all human beings—in the eye of the new-born baby—is blue.

That colour is as blue as the sea that came before the earth.

Blue as the sky itself that came before both.

For a long time, the Somme was just a little stream, as small as the one that flowed from the invigorating springs of Saint Marcoul.

Sar was the shaman who held the bay that the Somme formed in the North Sea within her power. Her seer's eyes were as blue as the eyes of new-born children. One evening, in the depths of her being, she heard in the distance Icelanders arriving in their boat. Among the Franks, only the women had a gift of second sight because, they said, only women are at the origin of both men and women—that is to say, of both children and the aged; that is to say, of both fantasies and ghosts.

Sar saw all that was going to happen as though it had already taken place. That was her gift. The Franks said:

'She sees everything. She can pick out a white hair that has fallen in snow. And if she takes it between her fingers, she can pick out one of those snowflakes on a white eyelash in a bowl of milk.'

Her eyes were blue, blue as corundum and sapphire.

Everyone noticed them, admired them and said: 'How blue her eyes are!'

Hartnid said: 'They are the bluest eyes in the world. They are as blue as the sky after the storm, when it is pure and shimmers upon the calm sea.'

The shaman's eyes enchanted him.

Yet suddenly, at certain moments, her eyes, grown cold and grey as granite, would set in a stare. She would see enemy troops a number of years into the future.

She would say: 'In three years, the enemy from the north will land. It will be raining. The river will be in spate and none of you will move, but remain sitting on the sea wall watching the water rise up to your knees. Then you will either meet your death from their blows or become their slaves.'

Sar the Shaman brought down on herself the laughter of the fishermen and the hunters and the metalworkers and the warriors of the Somme by warning them too far in advance of what was going to happen. It was never clear when the future she divined would suddenly come to pass. She was a prophetess who saw much too far into the future. Hence, when the events occurred, the Franks had forgotten the prophecy she had once made.

Furthermore, she drew protests from the oldest among them, as she spurred them to take precautions that invariably proved quite futile.

One rainy day, a day when, as they sat on the sea wall, the little river before their eyes was bursting its banks, the Norsemen, who came from the island of Iceland, attacked them. They killed most of the men who tried to defend themselves. They took into slavery the children and women, together with the old, decrepit, white-haired men in their dotage.

The Vikings asked the Franks, 'Do you not have a shaman, then, to predict calamities?'

It was then that the defeated Franks told them of Sar's prophecy. They remembered now that everything she had predicted in the most minute detail three years before had come about: the rain, the river bursting its banks, the knees getting soaked, the surprise attack, etc. Then the Norsemen asked where Sar lived. Under torture, one of the Franks who had been taken prisoner pointed out to the young Icelandic sailors where the shaman had chosen her cave in the cliffs. The Norsemen climbed the slope, drove away the gulls, entered the cave, drove out the bats, took her by the arm and put her eyes out. Her blue pupils flowed and flowed without end. This is how the Somme was created, which now sends its endless flow out into the North Sea, reaching as far as the port of London.

14. The Face

One evening a boat came down the river. The rower brought its black hull to shore among the little yellow, diamond-shaped leaves of the great willow trees of Hagus the ferryman. A most handsome man, notably slim and seeming like an angel, jumped on to the bank and signalled to someone out of sight.

The boat set off again in silence.

The two men walked along the bank.

The first of them soon became known to everyone. They were aware that he was called Hartnid and he was looking for something. He was looking for a face. He had a little enamel box in his shirt. He opened it. It showed a face that had been painted on a Scottish island and he asked: 'Have you seen this face?' It was the face of a woman who wasn't particularly beautiful but had an air of great gentleness about her. The man was called Hartnid and from time to time a jay with blue wing-feathers would come and sit on his shoulder.

II

(The Book of the Inscrutable Heart)

1. The Secret Chamber

There is a hidden room in the women's house where they give birth. No man is entitled to enter. That is where the renewal of Frankish society takes place. The Mothers, known also as the Sources, jealously guard its secret. They pass this on to their daughters in adolescence and, from that day onwards, girls cease to be girls, their flow begins and they become women. Berehta (Bertha), the daughter of Karel (Charles), was one of these mothers. *Cor inscrutabile*—that was the Latin sobriquet Hartnid was given by his mother, for Jeremiah had written in his prophecies (Jeremiah 17:9): *Pravum est cor omnium et inscrutabile quis cognoscet illud* (The heart of all men is depraved. It is inscrutable. Who could know it?).

John was called the eagle, since he prophesied.

Nithard was called the goose, since he was constantly writing in every tongue.

Hartnid might have been called the horse, so much did he wander, so much did he ride, and so fond was he of their beauty, impetuosity, bulk, grace, manes and genitals, but, because of what his mother had said, he was called inscrutable heart.

2. The Hunting Dog called Hedeby

Coastal Duke Angilbert's hunting dog barks and throws out its front paws. The bitch turns around. The hound mounts the hindquarters that the bitch presents to him, clings on to her backbone as far as he's able, clings on vigorously—for all that he's worth—with his front paws. He penetrates her from behind, continuing for some time.

One day in 807, in the inner courtyard at Aix-la-Chapelle, Emmen, daughter of Emmen, is watching this coupling. To Hartnid, who is standing by her side, she says: 'It's horrible with dogs. With men, too, it's horrible.'

'Did you see what he did?' young prince Hartnid asked Princess Emmen.

'Yes.'

Hartnid blushed beside her. He was nine years old at the time.

'I've never seen a man do to a woman what Hedeby did to that unfortunate animal.'

The princess went on: 'Here's how it seems to me. It's only marvellous among horses. Mounting is something that suits only horses. Have you, Hartnid, ever seen a finer member than that of a horse when it swells, bends and hardens? Have you looked on finer hair than the mane of a wild horse floating behind its head as it runs through the barley, thistles, moss, broom, rocks and lichen that cover the moors?'

3. Aude's Waiting Maid

In a village belonging to the Abbey of Stavelot, the fields of spelt, cabbages and wheat formed a semi-circle.

Then they all stopped suddenly, like an amphitheatre of cereals and vines, at the thoroughly gloomy, thick, bushy, wild, tangled forest of the Ardennes.

A forest so dense, dark, ancient and primal that no one dared pass into it without taking precautions and sewing two or three talismans into their clothes.

It was from there that wild boar would suddenly rush out in hordes.

They would ravage the fields, fruit trees, vines and vegetable plots in the time it took for an April shower to fall, for a lightning bolt to strike.

Even when, further along, the heathland of Chooz came to a stop at the Meuse, opposite that—just a few yards away—it was still the cliff-face of the forest that the river ran up against.

And it was even more impenetrable.

They called this place Le Trou du Diable—the Devil's Hole.

The clouds languished up in the sky.

The clouds lay heavy for days and days above the village of the monks of Stavelot Abbey.

The clouds were more or less imprisoned by the loop of the river, on account of the steep cliff face.

A cliff face too smooth to get a handhold on.

A rock impossible to climb.

The clouds clung to the thorns, held fast to the treetops which they watered with rain for months on end.

Lucilla said shyly: 'I knew Aude and served her.'

Hartnid said: 'She's been gone fifty years. They said of you that you were in fact the daughter, by another woman, of the prefect Roland.'

'That's true.'

'You're clever. You're beautiful.'

She was uneasy. She tried humour: 'I already see more clearly what I can bring you. But you, what would you bring me in exchange for my cleverness and beauty?'

'My courage and my fear.'

'I'd only be happy with the first half.'

'It's all of a piece.'

'The first half could have been the whole of it, if you'd worked at that.'

'Not at all, because my fear isn't fear that my courage might fail. At the request of the caliph who governs Saragossa, the Frankish tribes have gone to fight a new war against the assaults of the emir who reigns over Cordoba. I am merely a half-prince. A bastard prince. But it isn't weariness of military operations, nor mountain snows, nor the violence of battle, nor the death I might suddenly meet in war that I'm afraid of.'

'Then be more precise when you speak of your fear.'

'When I come back, you'll tell me if you want me. That you might not consent to become my wife—that is my fear.'

'And if I don't want you even now?'

'I've just told you, that's my fear.'

'Yes, but if I phrase my question another way, what will your answer be, bastard prince? What will your thinking be if I haven't waited for you?'

'If you haven't waited for me, I shan't disturb the course of the existence you'll then be leading. On the other hand, if you stay patient . . .'

'I shall not wait for you.'

She said that, but she grasped his hand and squeezed it, squeezed it very tight.

She didn't let it go right away. Then she turned her back on him and walked away, departing at speed.

Her fragrance left with her.

He remained there alone, his hand searingly hot.

And something invisible around his face, which was what lingered of her perfume.

He glanced at the boat's guardrail and stepped over it, without using the hand she had touched with her marvellous one.

He looked at the water.

Then he turned around to look at the riverbank and saw the figure of Lucilla receding into the distance.

After a time, he opened the hand that the woman had squeezed longer than necessary and raised it to his eyes. He hid his eyes behind that hand which she had seared by touching it. Then, behind the back of that hand, he began to cry. He sat down on the thwart. He cried his heart out. That was the fear in the depths of his being. The uncontrollable tears were his fear. The fragility in the face of what he loved: that was his only fear, but it was immense. From childhood, he had seen only cold—and, at times, infuriated faces—annoyed by his presence, irritated by his desires, wearied by his being a child, and he would go off and sob far away from those stern gazes.

Only his twin, Nithard, knew of his tears, watched over his withdrawings, covered for his absences, but said nothing.

He protected him but gave him no reassurance.

Hartnid sobbed for as long as he was away from the harsh gaze of the world. Then he went off to Aramitz, to Hasparren, crossed the Adour river, went beyond the pic de Bigorre and down towards the red earth of Spain.

She waited six years for him. She saw a corpse return.

The corpse could still speak a little.

'I waited for you,' she told him.

'You were wrong to do so because very little has returned.'

'Does that very little still love me?'

'I love you.'

'Then I shall marry you, for I have waited for you also and I love you too.'

The tears welled up into his eyes, gushed from his eyelids and he let them flow in silence before her.

Lucilla took his scrawny face in her hands and caressed his prickly, hollow cheeks, damp as they were.

'You won't weigh heavy on my belly, Hartnid,' she mumbled.

Not only did she marry him but they were happy together.

4. The Bilberry Man

Now, one day long ago, at the end of winter, the Bilberry Man (*Heidelbeermann*) offered Hartnid a tiny little berry that had gone bad; it was dirty, foul smelling, pinkish, purplish. Hartnid took it delicately in his fingers and wanted to make a gift of it to the woman he loved. This latter, called Lucilla, made the mistake of rejecting it with distaste. That is why men suffer death.

One day, the Bilberry Man said to Hartnid: 'If you want to steer clear of death, you have to go down on your knees each evening, at the foot of your bed of bracken or straw, and inwardly recite the rhyme that goes with bilberries.

But, since no one has ever known the words of the bilberry rhyme, that custom has fallen into abeyance.

The woman said no to the berry. The bird came and sat on her shoulder. Hartnid departed.

5. The Mark on the Wall Left by Hugh the Bell-Ringer

One day long ago, in 811, at the monastery of St Richarius, Count Angilbert's head forester died from an ill-intentioned axe blow that severed his neck. Why? That remains a mystery. The priest who had charge of the day's services asked Frater Lucius to run as fast as he could and fetch Hugh the master bell ringer from the village.

Lucius knocks on the door so that he can tell the bell ringer he will have to sound the death-knell.

His wife comes out of the little house.

She gazes with astonishment at Frater Lucius as he explains what has brought him.

Hugh's wife says to the friar: 'Do you know, Lucius, Hugh told me he was with you at the abbey.'

'No, that's not right.'

'I can see that.'

'I was labouring at a copy all morning and was never away from my oak stool.'

'Then we're going to see something I find personally disgusting.'

'I am not keen to,' replied Brother Lucius.

'Never mind whether you're keen or not. Please follow me.'

She doesn't bother to close the house door behind her. She treads on the tail of the ginger cat stretched out on the threshold. It squeals and jumps in the air. She tugs at the sleeve of the monk's robe and repeats: 'Follow me, vicar.'

'I'm not a vicar, I'm a monk. I like cats and I don't think you have the right to mistreat them.'

'I mistreat whom I like and you'll see whom I mistreat.'

She drags Brother Lucius behind her and comes to the archer who is standing at his watchman's post at the end of the little street. She grabs him by the arm.

'I need you and your weapon. Follow me, archer.'

All three make for the town square.

'Are you sure our presence is necessary,' asks the archer.

Suddenly she gestures to them to be quiet.

The bell ringer's wife takes off her clogs.

She holds them in her hand as she crosses the cold cobblestones in silence.

Suddenly, she points out Hugh, who is inside a tavern drinking with a girl.

At that moment, the chief bell ringer turns his head and sees his wife just as she sees him. He runs off so suddenly and with such terror and haste that his shadow remains stuck to the tavern wall. Even when he was dead, even after his body was buried (at Soufflenheim eight years later, in 819, after the wedding ceremony of King Louis the Pious and Judith Welf, princess of Bavaria), his shadow was still stuck to the wall. People still pointed to it and said: 'It's the bell ringer's shadow. He left so quickly that he hadn't time to take it with him.'

The story, famous among the Franks, does not end here.

A Saxon painter by the name of Creekevild, a man of Aix-la-Chapelle (Aachen), saw that shadow on the tavern wall one day when he had come there to drink and enjoy himself.

6. Origin of the Shadow of Saint-Riquier

One day long ago, a painter at the Palatine Court who came from the Palatine spa town of Aix-la-Chapelle (Aachen) with the intention of painting the vault and oculus of the crypt that goes down to the spring of Saint Marcoul beneath the abbey church of the first Frankish king Richarius (Riquier), discovered this shadow on the wall of the village tavern that stands beside the abbey close. He had the idea of making a world out of it. Creekevild the Painter did not touch the dark patch that the flight of the bell ringer had left on the wall. To him it seemed like an emblem of a farewell to this world, particularly as it is the remnant of such a farewell. The shadow of a horror prompting an escape—the very escape all monks make from the world. He was careful not to draw the slightest line on it. He didn't spread even the lightest of colour on it. He simply let it be, interpreting it as a lake full of mysteries. He painted two shores around it: one with a swan coming over to enter the water; the other with a unicorn arriving to drink. Above them, a string of willows leads to a spring. A queen, who seems to be Herminia or a goddess, in this case closely resembling Arduinna, is fleeing the Christian horsemen who pursue her. She looks back, into the distance, at the black line of the dark forest. First we see her stooping, slipping beneath the branches. Then she is galloping through the forest. She throws off her pursuers, but does this so quickly that she herself gets lost as she tries to give them the slip.

Afterwards, she roves around for a long time not knowing what direction she is going in and not guessing where she might be heading. Gradually, the darkness fades. She comes up to a shelter made from stones the goatherds have piled up on the mountainside. It is dawn. The droplets of the dawn are all around. She dismounts. She falls asleep near the water of the spring that leads to the black lake, which is wholly devoid of any hint of living beings. The gushing water thrusts its little waves against the bank covered with little lilies, amid the song of the birds that are beginning to stir. Then comes the shrill sound of the musettes of eight little goatherds, who arrive among the poplar trees and merrily play a tuneful response to the birdsong. They discover the beautiful sleeping horsewoman. They take out the mouthpieces of horn and approach the sleeping goddess of the forest. They see her two splendid breasts gently rising. They are stunned by the lustrous sheen of her hair, like threads of gold: they fall silent before it. All eight of them sit down to watch her breathing and sleeping. They cease their ritornello. They have abandoned their eight reed-pipes at her feet. They weave eight baskets as blond as the queen's hair that shines out around her closed eyelids. A stag approaches slowly, seven feet tall. The goats and the eight little goatherds guarding them rise and part to let it pass. The five-pronged stag comes and examines the young woman's horse, which bends its neck towards it as a mark of fealty, before calmly turning away. The horse isn't in the least afraid of the stag. The great stag slowly lowers its antlers and comes and drinks beside the goddess Arduinna, sleeping in the depths of her own forest. The stag laps the water that shines among the pebbles on the shore, then falls to its knees. Then the goddess opens her black eyes—eyes blacker than the crows that guard the sun. She weeps, and in this way everything returns to that water which flows into the dark lake of the Origin where it is born. For it seems that this mysterious water that runs down the faces of men goes back there sometimes, while it is possible that in the depths of every living being it merely dries out. I have known many men in whose depths that water had evaporated.

7. Appearance of Saint Veronica in the Bay of Menton

There was also a mark that was left on a piece of cloth. A man was so afraid of his imminent death that a woman of low standing wiped his face in a Jerusalem alleyway with the veil she wore over her hair. John wrote in his Book: *Primum caelum et prima terra abiit et mare jam non est. Prima abierunt. Et ego Johannes vidi.* (Sky and earth fell away and the sea was no more. Then I, who bore the name John, saw and then I understood that the Origin was coming undone.)

All the things that had been the first to emerge on the Earth's crust after they had sprung from the water were being annihilated one after the other.

In the distance, in a sort of fog that began to form over the sea, one could see a lost woman rising up behind the external world, which had also vanished, along with the primal presences and the different gleams of light.

It was a shade that held in its hands a face that it bore on its belly.

It was thus that Saint Veronica, come from the—oh so fragile—temple that overlooks Jerusalem, silently appeared in the waters of the Bay of Menton.

A majestic, wandering dead woman, her smile full of sadness, her robe filled with shadow, grew in stature on the banks of the Acheron as the mud sucked her under.

The foul waters were up to her thighs.

She hitched up her tunic and, encircled by delicate, silky, moist, sparkling, soft blond hairs, one could see not the face of a god but a little black hole that implacably drew one's gaze.

O Prostitute, who go hither and thither, opening yourself to the excited shades, who utter little moans to gain access to the other world!

We men merely slip a little grey fish into your darkness.

8. The Road to Louviers

I was born in country where all the names ended in 'bec' or 'beuf'. 'Bec' was the stream. 'Beuf' was the hut. Tourlaville referred to the farm of Thorlak. I lived in Verneuil opposite the ruins of a church dedicated to Saint John the Evangelist. In those times, the word Louviers didn't mean a lair of wolves, but 'ancient place'. At Vernon, near the collegiate church, there still stands a fine, ancient house with wooden corbels which has a magnificent Annunciation of the Birth of the Lord. That house, which long served as an inn, is called Le Temps Jadis, Days of Yore.

9. Silent Theodrada Turns Around and Sees Bertha and the Coastal Duke

The woman turned around. She looked at the man she loved who was speaking to her older sister. Then she observed her friends and the princes and the servants and the slaves all around her. All eyes were shunning this world, turning away from it. But no matter: she loves this man who is speaking with her sister. She furtively leaves the court to follow them. They hasten away and come to the spring that lies beneath a stone arch. There are large, heavy clusters of wisteria hanging along the wall. She sees her sister grasp his member and pull back its fleshy covering; the strange snake throbs between her fingers and she puts it into herself.

10. On Our Miraculous Lives

In stories dating back to ancient times, there is often mention of great wonders. It isn't that there are fewer such wonders these days intervening—quite as unexpectedly as before—in the course of our lives. But their occurrence doesn't register in the mind as it did in days of old, when, in the repetition of the tasks of ordinary life, nothing new really made calls upon it.

The memory of their surprising nature also fades because we are wary of noting them in family records, in *res gestae*, in chronicles, in private diaries, in history books, in engagement books.

So miracles seem less frequent to us, when in fact the world abounds with them.

Many ascetics take the road to paradise, but it is true that they have given up bearing witness to their deliverance these days. They are wary of their fellow human beings. Why would they speak of their happiness? They would be afraid of stirring up jealousy. They remain secretive and concentrated in their solitude, in which their serenity itself intensifies right up to the moment when they die, without their being separated from it for a second. The wave remains in the depths of their being. It doesn't rise to their eyelids. They probably love their happiness more powerfully than the men of Antiquity. The enormous joy of the last moments of their lives is something they protect from the world even more.

11. On the Euphoria of Men and Women

For in days of yore, when we were coming to a climax of joy, we used to hold our breath.

And the pleasure, which then overtook us, was increased.

Here is the reason for this, according to the words of Saint Anselm in the sermon to which he gave the title of the psalm *Animam reprime*!—Restrain the soul. That sermon is perhaps the finest homily Christian friars ever wrote in their history.

To await one's climax is to await an extraordinary access of faintness, without knowing at what moment it will arrive.

The body is not even certain that this elation or this fall will occur.

There is no way for women or men to prepare themselves for what will occur or eventuate. It is a faintness we can meet only with wide-eyed surprise, as our eyes close of their own accord and plunge us, in one single bound, into a darkness quite different from that of night. What is happiness other than a sinking? There is no joy that does not have a trace of unpredictable faintness. Such is the homily I wished to deliver to you today, my brothers. Restrain the soul, as God did Himself, until the cry came that was merely a cry of abandonment. Then to His lips the Ancient tongue returned! But I do not wish to speak before you at any greater length of this obliteration into the absolute blackness that lies at the bottom of the world, for he who speaks of it is carried off by it!

12. Macra

Lean did you enter and lean also will you leave this sojourn. Your face is nothing more now than your brow and a twinkling eye. Your hair? A tenuous memory of your childhood.

'There is nothing around my ears now but vanished voices!'

Sar spoke up and replied to Hartnid: 'Don't look at me in the light! I have no face now that looks like me! My eyes are put out! I have bitten on the hook of death! When? I shall have to search among my memories. At what moment did the traps open, to have closed again so swiftly on my days?

'It wasn't night. The waters of the bay were awash with *knarrs* and *drakkars*. The soldiers were killing the monks and the abbots. The count was rolling about in the water.'

'Here is the truth. The questions are three. Where "where?", when "when?", why "why?"'

'I don't see what you are saying.'

'Then I shall put the question that haunts me now another way, a way which perhaps brings all the questions together. Why, as I was in my cave up on the cliff, while you had your feet in the water, fighting courageously against the swords and the oars and the lances and the axes, were all the questions closed off and, as it were, sealed up, without my being aware of it? Why has nothing interested me any more since you went to where my eyes no longer see—into the invisible?'

13. St Augustine's Sermon on Love

Saint Augustine said it was the same with the light that suddenly bathed our faces when we were born as it was with the love in which they were made. 'O my brothers!' he suddenly exclaims from up in the pulpit in the great Roman basilica of Carthage, 'In truth, I tell you, love is not primary! Love struggles as best it can against the hatred of all that is other. All that is unknown to it leaves it distraught and readier to flee it than embrace it. Love is like a child that is frightened of the stranger who enters his father's house. Love contains as best it can the aggressiveness that threatens its eyes which are now wide open in horror. Those eyes are not so much fascinated by what they see as by the fear of seeing. When a body desires a body, the impatience that possesses it curbs as best it can the violence it inflicts in the violation with which it ends. But that is merely a curb. It is just a holding-in-check. There is anger in desire, just as there is nothing but destruction in hunger. Where are the little velvety, dull, pimply red fruits of the raspberries, where are the dark, bloom-covered bilberries, where are the golden seeds of the bunches of grapes after you have slipped them between your lips? They descend into a darkness I cannot express. Where is the hind that ran about the clearing at the crack of dawn? And where the young rabbit that frolicked so happily all night on the grass of the heathland? Once they have left the succulent fragrance of the charcoal over which they are roasting, a darkness I cannot express closes over them. So it is not the light that is filtered in the half-light where lovers mingle, when the one raises her dress above her face and the other lowers his breeches to his feet. It is the primal darkness that precedes us that then comes over them, as it does over us. It is the night of our mothers that gradually creeps over the bodies we denude: rising in an immense wave, it returns with an inexplicable force over the body that was conceived once in that darkness and which it still envelops. Then lovers shut their eyes very tight to find greater pleasure and let themselves be swallowed up entirely in the old world, which calls on their souls to dissolve completely and to melt into it.'

III

(Wo Europa anfängt?)

1. The Mountain Passes of the Pyrenees

When the Franks had to fall back from Spain, when the emir who reigned over the city of Cordoba renounced the cooperation he had requested from their king, when Uthman ibn Ali Naissa broke the agreement he had struck with Duke Odo, when the warriors and horses and waggons completed their forced march across the Pyrenees back to France, the men leading them were not minded to sing. They spoke quietly to their divine beasts to ask them to advance cautiously along the paths, they pulled them on gently by their reins, they clung to the rocks.

Firs are the favourite trees of the clouds.

They reach up spontaneously towards them. The clouds come, revolve around them, move in and batten onto them. Suddenly, they press down on them. They are sure companions and, certainly, wonderful lovers. Tree tops, boles, trunks and the bark around them, raise themselves higher to grasp their mysterious substance and cling on to it. Then the clouds enfold them in dampness in a passionate—or at any rate such a frequent, recurrent—way.

They return, grow heavier, flow. They are faithful.

They hate the light.

They love the snow, which the sky mysteriously creates.

When they were halfway into the clouds, the bare faces of the Franks and their long hair had become invisible; the magnificent manes of the horses were also invisible now.

At Roncevaux Pass, on 15 August 778, which was the Feast of the Assumption, in the warm cloud that had turned to mist, Eggihard the seneschal, Roland the Prefect of Brittany and Anselm the Count of the Palace died from slingshot wounds inflicted by the Basques.

2. Goddesses of Birth

When Aude was informed that Roland the Prefect of Brittany was dead, the blood drained from her face, she spun round three times from the right and fell on her left side, as Our Lord would fall on his own face on the last day on the Mount of the Skull.

She was dead.

Sar prophesied:

'Goddess, you no longer have your hunter!

Leave us, Goddess, since the immortals are not allowed to see death!

Similarly, you did not have the boldness to face up to the desire of your priest,

He who was called Aktaion,

You were not able to face his manhood that he raised towards you,

Strange goddess that is so afraid of desire,

For want of being able to look upon death!

O woman, you who want to see of the world only birth and children!'

3. Hartnid, Loves

The higher the mountain rises, the more it comes into contact with the cold of the sky. The more it breaks up from the effect of freezing, the more the tips of its rocks snap away and the more the ice fragments those rocks. The debris rolls down the slopes; the rains bore into them; torrential streams scar the most imposing masses of stone, before scouring them down. Snow sliding from the peaks piles up lower down and forms glaciers which themselves push and press against the cavities that hold them. Gradually the glaciers form these into corries or cwms from which rivers flow. Last, the rivers slowly hollow out the immense furrows of the valleys down below the mountainsides.

This is how mountains rise and nature sculpts itself.

Thus the bulkier the outcrop, the steeper its height, the greater is the erosion and the more the mountainside is hacked into and the more torrential and white is the streaming of the waters.

The fragment in this world is the lightning flash.

Seen from afar, the water rushing down through the pines seems as white as the snow covering the mountain top.

Once upon a time, beyond the mountains, in the Arab land of Andalusia, there was a two-year-old black mare that Hartnid revered.

For a time, he turned his back on the love of men, ceased to love women and abandoned his jay: he became passionate about horses. Throughout that time, Prince Hartnid followed the example of Saint Hippolytus, who had wished to die with his horses in the sea: their faces seemed more handsome to him than the bare, flat, frightened faces of humans.

Hartnid came to revere the ancient hero whose love was all for the woods, the forest, the sea shore, dunes and heathland.

At that time, he was entranced by chaos and collapse, by caverns and their vaults, by echoes and by wind buffeting the mountains.

Hartnid took as his model the one who preferred solitude above all things: his hand sufficed for his joys and even made them more imminent to the point where he sang.

Hartnid didn't hesitate to declare himself in love with Artemis: the nudity and the silence surrounding her captivated him more than sensual delight with its agitation and cries.

In the end, he became a lover of the wild: the Origin had a greater call on him than any bliss that was to come, even greater than the eternity which the group contended would be the lot of Christian knights at the end of Time.

Saint Hippolytus once said: 'Each person has only his part of the world. Crowds are made for courts as fish are for water. As birds prefer to rise into the infinite changeableness of the sky. As the bounding felines sit apart to lick their fur, alone, in their silence, casting a wary eye on those who come near them, I am wild at heart. I am like the hydrangea that prefers its shady corner. I am like the buzzard that barely betrays the site of its nest with its cry. I abandon speech to those who lie and to the old dead women who invent for themselves destinies they have not had in order to draw you into their arms. Nowhere is there a man who has sought less to deceive anyone in the world, to feign anything whatever, because, to put it simply, he has rejected contact with the world. I do not love you, Father. I do not love men. Nor did I covet your wife, Father: I shied away from women. I know nothing of the postures of love, except what I have seen in paintings on the portico walls. I did not wish to take your palace from you and to have it before it was my due. All your suppositions are absurd and vainly designed to abase me. There are too many guards, maidservants, faces, too much lamentation and strife for me ever to reign in your residence. I neither like being looked at nor observed and judged by lingering eyes. I don't like cities, the power that humiliates, the servitudes that degrade and the orders that fill people with anger or resentment. I love solitude, horses without bit or bridle, without reins, without saddles, without shoes. I love their magnificent bodies. I love the water that flows by, the water you dive into, from which you emerge new and naked, as on the first day when you catch yourself discovering that you are always being born.'

4. On Prince Bellerophon

He who fell headlong from his horse
(*ab equo praeceps*)
lost his eyes
and broke his legs
died a fine death,
met his end
in Aleia,
like Hyppolitus in the shifting sand
like his head rolling in the waves of the sea.

5. The Lantern on the Tigris

In 778, the Prefect Roland died on a mountain side, his back
against a pine tree, his horse already dead.

In 778, at the very moment when, in the middle of the
month of August, the Prefect of Brittany breathed his last, as
night was falling gently on his palace grounds, Caliph Harun
al-Rashid suddenly felt a sense of panic seize his throat.

He began to howl. He called his vizier, Jafar the
Barmakid, and told him: 'I have to go out. I can't sleep. I'm
terribly restless. There's a pain inside me, tearing me up!
Let's get out of the palace!'

They dressed; from their slaves, whom they ordered to
strip, they took poor men's clothing, so as not to be
recognized; they left by the guards' tunnel, coming out on
the banks of the Tigris.

On the Tigris they spotted an old man in a boat and hailed him.

'What's your name?'

'Hagus,' said Hagus.

He was very old. He had difficulty turning his head towards them.

'Take us, Hagus, in the darkness of evening, on to the river. Light your lantern. Take this dinar for your pains and this other for the oil in your lamp.'

'No. Who would be so bold as to sail on the river with lights lit while Harun al-Rashid reigns over this world?'

Harun al-Rashid opened up his coat and, beneath his poor man's rags, his robes were resplendent as a sun.

'If you do not obey my order, you will die.'

The boatman, who was very old, stroked his white beard. He did not think for very long, as Caliph Harun al-Rashid struck him a violent blow.

Then Hagus got back unsteadily to his feet on the deck of his boat. He lit his lantern and, with some difficulty, hung it on the hook that was nailed to the mast, sat down on the bench at the back of his boat and grabbed the tiller. And so, in the darkness, they sailed along the banks of the river till dawn.

When they came back, Mazrur, the Baghdad executioner, beheaded the old boatman called Hagus.

6. Beneath the Left-Hand Wheel
of the Women's Cart

There isn't just the story of the Count of Vannes, Hruodlandus, Prefect of Britanny, beside his dead horse, who blew for all he was worth into an olifant that made not the slightest sound. There aren't just the wonderful tales which at times, when night has come, ease the insomnia of the Caliph Harun al-Rashid at the point when the sun is disappearing and anxiety tightens his throat. There is also a strange legend told of the King of the Franks on his return from Spain, when he found himself in the foothills of the Pyrenees and was marching at the head of his army in the August heat. The troops are advancing along a stony path. Suddenly the emperor sees a little tree-frog jump from stone to stone across the dusty path. The Emperor Charlemagne also howls, like Caliph Harun al-Rashid, but among the Franks 'howling' means something quite different. Howling, in the language of the Franks, means making the sound that wolves make.

The emperor howls, then tugs on his horse's bridle. He brings it to a halt.

He howls a second time, for the women's cart, which is following him, to stop immediately.

He genuinely makes the full-throated cry of a wolf.

Sadly, his howling, or rather his second 'wolf's bark' is uttered in vain.

As if turned to stone, the emperor stares at the tiny crushed frog on the other side of the iron-rimmed left wheel that stands gleaming on the path.

The whole army has come to a standstill. The emperor on his horse is sobbing.

Theodrada gets out of the cart and walks over to her father: 'Do not cry, Father. You'll find hundreds like this one in the pools and lakes.'

'There are perhaps many frogs in the pools and lakes but it was this one I failed to save,' replied Charles to his daughter Theodrada.

His daughter Gisele (Giseldrudis) comes over and grasps her father's hand. His daughter Emmen stands stiffly by him, saying nothing.

His daughter Berehta comes over in her turn, crouches down and takes the little brown victim in her fingers.

'I'm going to put it in a bowl of water. I'm going to look after it. Perhaps it will recover?'

'It is flattened and naked.'

'All frogs are flat and all frogs are naked.'

'Once again, this frog isn't all frogs.'

'I'll give it cress to eat,' says Gisele.

'I'll give it little berries which I'll go and gather from the mountain and I'll prepare them with my own hands with a little milk,' says Emmen.

'I've a bad feeling about this,' says the emperor to his daughter Berehta, 'for it seems to me that it is dead'.

In the evening when they had made camp and everyone was sleeping, he went to see the sick frog in its bowl in his daughter Bertha's tent. It was still dead. It was already withered.

Then the emperor announced: 'As night fell and the moon rose, I was looking for you just now in the bushes and beneath the spindly trees that cling to the hillside between the rocks. Nowhere did I find your like.'

Then he thought of his grandson called Hartnid.

Now, his daughter was standing behind him in the shade of the tent.

'Stroke it,' his daughter suggested.

The emperor lifted from the water the little frog that had been crushed beneath the wheel of the women's cart and took it in his hand.

Its arms were stretched wide.

Its fingers were tiny.

He had difficulty making it out in the darkness.

He left the tent, still stroking the little tree-frog, its arms outstretched in the palm of his hand.

He viewed it in the light of the moon, which was full.

Then he smiled.

'We are not all fragments of a sword,' mumbled Berehta.

Einhard related this story in the *Vita* he wrote at Seligenstadt in 831.

7. The Siren's Song

Suddenly he heard the shrill cry of the Siren. He held the tiller straight. He drew closer. The bird came and flew over Hartnid's head but something of his mother—or rather of an older woman within him—whispered, 'Sail by without stopping!' He was, in any case, a man who never in his whole life thought of stopping. He sailed twice round the Isle of Sirens, then off again. Some moments later, he let go the tiller. He gave the vessel up to the motion of the waves. He let the wind guide him.

8. On the Cheeks, Ears and Silken Hairs of Love

The governor of Barcelona, who was called Sulayman ben Al-Arabi, decided to leave the Bilad-al-Ifrang (the Land of the Franks).

Sar immediately sang this song on love:

'It begins with more frequent glances.

One day, circumspectly, slowly, shyly, furtively, mutely, fingers dare to place themselves for a second on the forearm of the other body that is before one's eyes.

Another day, the palm of the hand forms something like a shell that closes over the back of the hand she is looking at

and the hand beneath the hand does not pull away.

Suddenly, bodies become mysteriously closer at a stroke, without their moving together in any way.

One day, they seem close forever, without their needing to move.

Then the mouth comes closer to the ear, to which you want to tell everything.

The mouth slips into the hair, red and black, where it whispers.

The lips come up against a sort of silk but avoid touching this strange shell.

One day, lastly, the gaze lingers over a part of the body which stands for all the parts of the body.

That day is the one day when there is love.

That day, clothing feels heavy.

That day, the body is so hot it seems on fire. A liquid flows in the depths of the eyes. A flush rises from down in the legs and runs over the belly, up beyond the navel, reaches the torso, moves up to the breasts which it tenses, rising into the eyes, which it widens. The voice lowers. Wrists work free of sleeves, fingers reach into the air that glides between bodies; they untie bows, remove clasps, undo buttons, open and caress. They grasp that which is agreeable to the touch.'

9. The Bird Catching the Fish

There was a great stone image set up on the plateau, gnawed at by the wind.

It showed a curved-beaked bird of prey catching a fish.

'Christ saving a sinner,' explained Frater Lucius to the young Prince Nithard as he was instructing him.

If Hartnid loved horses, Nithard was in love with birds, just as his grandfather had a fondness for the eagle, the falcon, the tercel, the goshawk, the gyrfalcon, the hobby, the merlin.

Frater Lucius loved the black kitten he had found on the path in the Saint Marcoul forest, the kitten that had made the tiled roofs of the cells and of the penthouses above the monastery gardens its domain.

The little cat brought the sparrows back one by one to its master.

Frater Lucius improvised this poem:

You great fevered swirling swarms that form
    strange letters in the sky
which God alone understands
before you finally disappear into the pale distance,
you are lost now in the curtain of rain that comes
    to us from the sea,
yet one day
you who fly off,
you who fly off to reach a farther isle which the sun
    indicates to you,
you who rise above the world of men until you
    disappear into the sky,
yet one day
you come back to the same niche in the stone.
to exactly the same place of shelter,
in the tiny corner
of the single springtime in time.

Hartnid loved a man one day for his hardiness.
Another day he loved a woman for her gentleness.
One day he loved a horse for its beauty.

One day he was at Cordoba. One day at Sens.
    One day at Reykjavik, one day at Glendalough,
    one day at Arklow, then at Dublin.
One day at Prüm and one day at Baghdad.
One day at Rome.
One day on the Bosporus beside the tower from
    which Leander threw himself into the Sea of
    Marmora.
Today he loves Limni.
But only the blue-tailed jay,
with its restless black crest, its terribly ugly voice
and its clear white rump,
the jay that so loves acorns that it prefers them
    to grain,
accompanies him wherever he goes,
opens its crooked beak to imitate his voice,
and leads him where its wings carry it.

10. The Farewell to the Mare of Limni

Hartnid replied to the old wizard woman, whose name was Sar, who never shifted from the cliffs of the Bay of the Somme, who sometimes set about his desire, as soon as it manifested itself, and satisfied it immediately in her mouth:

'Where do you see the rain as being something ill-starred?'

And before that, when he was still fourteen years old and she still had her unforgettable blue eyes, he replied to her:

'Give yourself to me and forget the seasons.'

And she answered him: 'Let the old she-wolf chop up the time in the same way as your beloved brother has to break it up. The way he has to organize it in portions for his king! To cut it up into exciting moments to lend verve to his *History*! I see him in the depths of time sitting at his desk! I already see him placing his boxwood-framed glasses on his nose! He is sitting like a lord by his young king, his two hands upon his leather-bound book!'

He answered her: 'Let his be the white quill of the goose and let me have the blue and black feather of the jay and the snow-white belly of the screech-owl! One last time, open your belly covered in white hairs and let me plunge myself into it! It is good, each evening, for the primary darkness within us to enshroud the world as it did before each of our births! For you know that I was the last-born, since, long ago, you brought us into the world!'

Old Sar, growing older as time went by, would let him have his say. She wouldn't let her feelings show on her face. Then, after she lost her sight, she would simply wait until the sound of his body had disappeared into the distance before weeping with her dead eyes.

When Hartnid left the mare of Limni forty years later, his voice wanted simply to talk to the wide winds. He exclaimed:

> O sands of the shore!
> O mountain forests where you passed by with your
>   slender dogs
> pursuing bears, dogs, men, stags, horses, lionesses,
>   desert panthers!
> No longer will you lead your Venetic mares,
> filling the arena of Limni
> with the galloping of colts being broken in!

It had grown bitterly cold. All the mares' little offspring had to be brought inside at Martinmas. He entrusted them to the domain's peasants. That done, he set off in pursuit of his jay, which had taken to following the wild geese in the sky.

11. Seneca's Circle

Poor pale hand, which from time to time comes into view—suddenly, curiously—when you're constantly writing with it but never notice it, even though it is only inches from the words you are setting down with black or red liquid ink.

One day the vine leaf, so supple, green and wide, is simply a piece of crumpled red paper—light, friable, insubstantial.

Poor ancient palm that no longer opens fully.

Poor crumpled leaf that still retains a little of the colour of blood.

Page so folded but so empty.

Armenian paper

which you twisted before bringing it up to the flame

and which smelt as good as the beloved clavicle and the delightful nook of the bone to be found where the tress of hair begins!

Triple lotus leaves knotted together and smoothed out on the banks of the Ganges.

Clay from between the two rivers. White Chinese papers. Umbels of the papyrus plant, at first clamped together, rolled and closed, but which one day open,

yawn,

immense crocodile jaws that come apart—dislocate themselves—like a great dark door on the surface of the pale water of the Nile

in unquenchable Hunger!

Hartnid and Nithard and Odo, Gregory and Fredegar, Alcuin, Hariulf, Angilbert, Eginhard and even, later, all the greats, Bernard, Abelard, Turoldus, Chrétien, Villon, Béroul, Renart, Froissart—the Frankish men of letters all had a maxim of Seneca the Philosopher on their lips, a maxim they were taught on their first day of study at the abbey schools which the emperor had founded between the Loire, the Yonne, the Seine, the Somme, the Canche, the Meuse and the Rhine, before adding many others to them.

It was a very curious thing, but each time they tried to quote it, the first maxim they had learnt would never rise to their lips, remaining inexplicably lost in the secret depths of their souls. It was like a word on the tip of your tongue that your breath could not locate, leaving the incisors and canines empty, leaving the strange life inside the skull bereft and anxious. Even Nithard, the most learned of them—or, at least, the first of them, since he was the first to write the language I am writing now, having invented that language by noting it down one evening in the camp erected on the snow on the banks of the river Ill—could recite it only with difficulty. He had to start over twice, as though he wasn't convinced, or as though he didn't want to mislay it so soon, as though he appreciated it without quite being able to make up his mind about it, or as though he were articulating it without understanding it, or, alternatively, as though he had first to copy it out word by word in his mouth to convince himself of the paltry meaning it expressed.

Yet Seneca's phrase, which the clerics and priests and abbots and bishops had such a struggle to remember was unadorned, cursory, ordinary, simple: *Cibus, somnus, libido, per hunc circulum curritur.* (Hunger, sleep, desire, that is our daily round.) Hunger, sleep and desire go round in our lives the way the ball of the sun describes a circle and returns each day with all flesh, human or animal, in pursuit. Such is the systematic time that affects our mouths, our heads, our bellies. The statement isn't false. Yet it isn't an extraordinary revelation either. But time after time Nithard, who was like the obsessed shadow of his brother, or the soul jealous of his adventure—Nithard, who was like a nest haunted by a vanished bird—forgot it.

For his part, Hartnid did what his twin found difficulty asking for, accomplished what he wore himself out vainly imagining, immediately effectuated all that met his desires.

The one twin yielded to the other the part that fulfilled his own dream.

The one wrote with his feet resting warmly on the lid of the box that held glowing embers beneath its iron grid. Alongside Brother Hariulf in his little cell. Alongside Brother Lucius, who transcribed the Greek with a little black kitten that climbed up on to his hand, lifted his goose quills, delicately pushed his knife to the edge of his desk and knocked it noisily to the ground.

The other sailed and rode, appeased his desires, his fears, his disgust, his shame at the other end of the world, on the other side of the world.

Cibus, somnus, libido, per hunc circulum curritur.

This, in the pure state, is the eminently simple life of cats that do their rounds, sleep and hunt.

It is simply a song that winds around, that goes around in your head as it carries the feet onward, casts shadows on the ground and offers its halts in time. A single urge drives the soul on endlessly. A voraciousness, a gluttony drive hatred endlessly and orient it. An impetuosity endlessly induces evil, which is that black liquor that man distils, re-boils, re-distils, improves, condenses, sublimates. Evil is to man—as Seneca again writes (he became something of a model for Nithard after Hartnid had gone to sea)—as black blood is to the squid, the black blood it emits to make itself invisible and survive in the depths of the water. Towards what does the beautiful tend? How can we dare to express it? What does it press towards? How can we not be averse to expressing it? Odo's head began to spin. Fredegar's mind was filled with horror. Alcuin was more reserved. Paul the Deacon felt a sort of fear. Gregory wasn't alarmed, but disapproved. Why is there an enormous code of religious prescriptions, of hunting magic, of peasant proverbs, of tricks of the trade, of family customs, of social obligations, of childhood prohibitions forming innumerable laws? Why an interminable list of venial offences and mortal sins, so as to restrain predation, to manage hunger, to limit thirst, to allow the land to rest and spare it from the plough, to repress sexual excitation, when all are pillaging, stealing, raping, burning, devouring, killing? How can we believe it would be possible to decide how one leads one's life divinely, or morally, or independently of the place—as contingent as it is spontaneous—where nature has us emerge, or aside from the genealogical entourage of the groups that breed there, or, lastly, apart from chance, fears and the possible? The lives of animals, human beings and birds are so basic. It's a tireless dark hunt that enchants and roams.

Like a wild race which repeats itself and sets the heart beating.

Which pants and sings.

12. The Wild Cascade

Out of the blue comes the sudden night-time cascade of four hoots from the little owl or the 'whoo-hoo-hoo-hoo' of the tawny owl.

This bird of the darkness is yet another cat and, on account of the strange whoo-hoo of the sudden call it makes as coldness begins to strip the trees of their leaves and take the earth in its grip, French calls this tawny owl a *chat huant* —a hooting cat.

This is why they say that it hoots, as they also say of it that it ululates, without deciding between the single and the double, between appearance and reflection, between the face and its twin, between Nithard and Hartnid, between the unique and the repeated.

The names of birds aren't merely conventional like the words of languages—which sometimes draw on them.

They derive from their calls.

Nor are faces precisely mere lines or features, like the signs of the different scripts—which often borrow from them.

The barn owl is called *chouette-effraie* in French—the scary owl—and its face does indeed *scare* all animals, whatever they may be.

Even ourselves!

Barn owl whose eyes are black agates, round and matt like eternity stones!

With its feathers the colour of tree bark, the back of the night-flying cat is invisible.

And this—hooting—tawny owl turns its back in order to sleep as soon as day breaks and, even if it sleeps right under our noses, *it turns its back on us so effectively* that we don't see it standing out against the bark, so absorbed is it into the background it has chosen in order to be present somewhere without being visible to hunters or sorcerers or bears or lynxes—so absorbed is it all day in its vaster dream.

A strange bird which, from the birth of spring, falls silent.

It is only from September to February—from the rain to the snow—that the hooting tawny owl hoots its strange 'whoo' in the deserted countryside.

As soon as the colours appear, as soon as the sun hoists itself into the celestial vault, the *chats huants* begin their silence.

In their days of loving, tawny owls hunt noiselessly in the half-dark. They bring back colonies of cockchafers and moths to the five little beaks that merely cry out, without yet hooting—without yet singing what never quite becomes a song.

13. Father Lucius and the Picture

It feels good to hang the picture of the one you love on your bedroom wall.

One day when he was alone in the evening, awaiting the return of his loved one, Frater Lucius took a piece of charcoal from his warming pan and drew the portrait of his cat on the wall of his cell.

He loved it so much that the image was perfect: from his wall, the little kitten sitting on its hind paws stared back at him with its beautiful black eyes.

To have the portrait of his friend in his room when the cat was out hunting in the warm night of a sunny day, when birdsong rang out on all sides luring it on, when that song gave it an even greater—swift, if erratic—desire to hunt than the pleasure of gorging itself, when it jumped from his arms to the floor, leapt onto the window sill and off into the semi-darkness, did not soothe his lover's longings, but eased his wait.

The day the abbot made his regular tour of the monks' cells, he had it scrubbed off.

A dismayed Frater Lucius went to see the abbot, who was also the duke of coastal Francia. He pointed out that he had taken infinite pains over the portrait of the little cat. He had made it so lifelike. He protested at the abbot's removal of it.

Saint Angilbert replied:

'Why do you complain about this and why should I feel sorry for you?'

'Because I loved that drawing, and in that drawing I love this cat.'

'In the Christian world which is ours today, it is not right to love black cats. I believe it may even be that they are evil incarnate with fur and a face.'

'That isn't true. Everything God made in Creation was good. There is nothing in it that portends evil.'

'Who said anything of portending evil?'

'Then, why, father, did you have it scrubbed off the wall?'

'Brother, to show affection for wild cats . . .'

' . . . it isn't a wild cat.'

'Where did you find it?'

'In the forest, where the arm of Saint Marcoul's river runs off towards the sea.'

'To lend one's affections to wild cats who live in the forest or to lynxes that live in the mountains or to bears that live in the caves is to concern oneself with the old demons and sprites. It is to prefer heretics and pagans to all the brothers who have become Christians. Why not shelter a poisonous, forked-tongued snake beneath your habit, or hide in your cell the beast with long black pincers that Latin calls *cancer*?'

A distraught Frater Lucius went to find Nithard, who heard his complaint and the replies his father had made to his former teacher.

He took the big magnifying spectacles with their light-coloured wooden frames and put them down on the desk at which he was reading; he leaned over and wiped his old master's tears.

Frater Lucius was the best copyist in the monastery. He knew Latin and read Greek better than any of the other monks in the abbey church's scriptorium. He had taught Hartnid and Nithard everything until the point when youth changed their bodies and other desires came to occupy their minds.

Nithard decided to intercede on his behalf with his father.

But Angilbert replied sharply to his favoured son, the first-born, the one he had given the name Nithard: 'Warn him, if he persists in this, to fear, rather, a pyre on the dunes on the banks of the Somme. I shall light the fire myself with armfuls of branches and twigs if necessary! I don't intend to have a wild, black cat numbered among my abbey's three hundred monks.'

Brother Lucius felt angry at the threat pronounced by the Duke of Francia. He began to detest him. He avoided Angilbert whenever he appeared at the end of one of the abbey's nine corridors. In the evenings, he begged his cat not to make its little hum and to tone down its mewing as much as possible, along with the purrs of satisfaction and pleasure it gave when it rubbed against him.

14. Alyla of Glendalough

From June to September, Hartnid thought only of her. Not for a single hour did he leave her. Their bodies were made for each other. Hartnid stayed at the domain of Glendalough until the grape harvest, participating in it with pleasure. For the young Irish girl he wrote two love songs, accompanying them on the zither. One September morning, he took her in his arms and told her he would leave before noon. Hartnid ate his meal and left. Alyla said nothing.

Before her family and friends, she did not cry. For years she said nothing. Her whole life long she told no one of her pain. She waited until she was alone in the chapel to weep— the chapel dedicated to the saints Eleutherius and Rusticus that Hartnid had had built—or out on the heath behind a bush or where a rock gave shelter from the wind.

Sometimes she was very distressed.

At those moments, life was hard. It seemed to her she had committed some wrong, hadn't sufficiently opened her arms to him, hadn't loved him enough.

At other times, she had the impression of a presence that felt good beside her; she walked with that presence by her side; spoke with that close to her as she skirted the shoreline.

At yet others, she made buckwheat pancakes with meat and slipped in lots of spices because Hartnid loved good food. And when he had stayed in the great house at Glendalough, he had appreciated them, savoured them, devoured them.

Then his shadow left her again for several seasons and Alyla was horrendously alone.

One night, after many long years, he came back. He came back very naturally in the silence of the night; she saw him again in her dreams, naked from head to foot. In the evening, he comes to warm himself against her body. She dresses carefully, differently, each time he approaches in the dark of night. She prepares herself. She covers her body with cream and massages it. She changes her undergarments. She plaits her hair. She puts on earrings. She slips bracelets on to her wrists. And not only does she see him again but she speaks to him and he replies. He explains that he is still looking for the woman he once saw but cannot find her.

She is happy that he has not found her.

She feels his presence near her in her bed. He genuinely warms the depths of her body, which at times has its flow. She wishes to be alone in her chamber at Glendalough. She loves that presence each evening. She presses her thighs together, draws her knees up to her chin and is happy. Almost happy.

15. Where Does Europe Begin?

Sar prophesied.

With Hartnid there, she sought to improvise this poem which bore on the continent that comes together in the West of this world and leads off towards the night:

> There is a goddess the bull has loved since the days
>   of clay tablets.
> Her name is Europa.
> Long ago, as a cow, she turned her back, opened
>   wide her hind legs and offered herself willingly
>   to the ardent manhood of the heavens.
> The old residents of Rome preferred to say that
>   Europa was a Phoenician princess who had
>   been abducted in Crete.
> But Europa's hooves never strayed as far as the
>   lands between Meuse and Rhine.
> She never stepped in the forests of the Ardennes.
> We have to tell the truth:
> In the course of her life,
> Europa only ever knew Istanbul and Ephesus.

16. Pain, Lucius

One day, Frater Lucius ran to the monastery library. He was a pitiful sight. An untidy mess. He was half-naked. He hadn't got his monk's habit on. His hair was unkempt. He looked like a madman. He ran barefoot across the flag-stones. And his big round spectacles weren't on the bridge of his nose. He was weeping his heart out. And as he wept, his whole body shook. He went to the wooden booth where Nithard was working on his *History*. He fell to his knees before him. He grasped the hem of the prince's robe.

'Come, come!' he said to his former pupil.

He was sobbing. Nithard got up and followed him. They walked through the Ambulatory that protected them from the rain. Frater Lucius pushed open the door of his cell which had been left ajar. The two of them went in.

Frater Lucius closed the door behind him and, pointing to it, began to scream.

The little black cat had been torn limb from limb.

Its head was hanging down to the left.

Its four paws were nailed to the wood like a sort of Christ—or at least a sort of little crow with red and black wings outstretched.

Its entrails hung down below its belly.

Frater Lucius screamed. He cried himself hoarse. He howled like a wolf as he gazed on his dead friend. His hair turned white on the spot.

IV

(The Book of Angilbert's Poem)

1. Prince Dagobert's Three Dogs

Having agreed that Dagobert should die, his brothers got
on their horses and chased after him. Dagobert was on foot
and they pursued him like a stag in the wild forest
surrounding the isle of Lutetia. They chased him as far as
the Mount of Martyrs (*Mont des Martres*), now called
Montmartre, in Lutetia. It was at that point that, in the
distance, deep in the wood below, in a clearing on the banks
of the river Croult, the child Dagobert spotted at his feet an
old ruined hermitage. It was there that Saints Dionysos and
Eleutheros, both natives of the city of Athens, had once
brought their heads to bury them amid the ferns, when they
had come down from the mount that was dedicated
to them.

Later, it was there that Queen Aregund was buried, so
greatly did she venerate the scholarly bishop Dionysos, who
wrote such beautiful books on silences, denial, nights,

ecstasies. Eleutherios copied out his homilies to the great empty God who lies beyond the stars.

Dagobert passed through the old gate that lay ruined amid the undergrowth.

Then, suddenly, the dogs following him came to a halt.

Neither the hounds, nor the troops, nor his brothers could enter the place, which seemed enchanted.

The little wild garden and the hut at its centre, extending down towards the source of the Croult, were surrounded by a magical protective screen.

The three dogs stood in open-mouthed silence at the line formed by the scrolls of the ferns.

The prince's brothers dropped spontaneously to their knees beside their dogs, which had fallen petrified on the banks of the Croult.

In 629, when Dagobert had become king of the Franks, he rebuilt these walls that had saved his life. He built a little church there above the tomb of Queen Aregund. He wished to be buried by her side.

This basilica was rebuilt by Abbé Suger, at which point it was given the name of the saint who had saved him from death.

2. The Red Cloth

One day long ago, on the heath of Gondalon, they saw a man sitting beside a big brown box by a pond, carrying a reed with a little bit of red cloth tied to the end of it.

Then they recognized him. It was the man with the box of performing frogs on his back.

On the other side of the pond, on her hands and knees, was a four-year-old girl called Aemilia, playing with the tadpoles, chasing after them with her fingers.

A dog called Keeper was by her side.

At that time, the pond bore the name Waters' Meeting.

3. The Origin of the Abbey of Saint-Riquier

Once the Abbey of Saint-Germain-des-Prés had been founded in 543, there was no end to the building of abbeys throughout the territory of the empire and their consecration to all the saints the Romans had persecuted in their arenas over centuries.

A knight withdrew to a hermitage above the Somme beside a holy spring dedicated to Saint Marcoul. He was called Richarius. His toga was covered with fleurs de lys. He had magnificent shoulders. He was so sturdy that he could carry a fully grown horse in his arms and cross rivers doing so. He was very handsome. He was so strong and pious and holy that everyone came to see him, fell to their knees in the mud among the mayflowers and the daisies and had themselves blessed by him, renewing their taste for life and their faith in it.

Not only did Richarius lay hands on them and remove their pain, but the water from his spring, which was dedicated to Saint Marcoul, was magically curative.

Not only did those who lived along the Somme come on foot in their droves, but the North Sea fishermen came too in their boats.

Not just Saxon monks, but Celtic druids.

And the princesses of the islands of Ireland came, their vessels in full sail, the prows carved with monsters.

As the number of pilgrims grew and grew, the hermitage turned into a monastery.

Some years after his death, it was a little village to which pilgrims came to touch the relics of the hermit king, going down into the crypt that was now too small for such crowds.

His thin, black body had gradually mummified beneath his fleurs-de-lys-studded tunic.

Men and women, lords and serfs lined up along the river of Saint Marcoul, patiently queuing back to the edge of the forest.

In the 790s, Charlemagne offered the monastery of Saint-Riquier to Duke Angilbert to turn it into a much larger abbey, build more chapels there, and make it worthy of the saint who gave it its name.

Here is how Angilbert, who knew the three holy languages, conceived his abbey:

He thought: 'God is Three.' So he had three churches built. He arranged them in a triangle and had galleries built to connect them.

He had thirty altars consecrated on the site.

He brought in three hundred monks.

In 802, Charlemagne, who was now emperor, made a present to the abbot, who was also his son-in-law, of his earliest ancient books on parchment, so that they could be copied in the scriptorium, decorated, illuminated, bound in leather and covered with precious stones.

Above the arches, Angilbert built a long library for Greek and Latin books.

4. Saint Florentius Hanging Up His Cloak

Saint Florentius' cloak isn't the cloak of Saint Martin. At the court of King Dagobert, when he was resident in his palace at Lutetia, Saint Florentius was constantly humiliated by the courtiers who had attached themselves to the king and deceived him openly and shamelessly.

One day, upon his arrival in the Great Hall, the counsellors and princes, his brothers, turned away as usual in disdain at this hairy monk, who always appeared with book in hand, shuffling his rope sandals across the flagstones. He was dressed as a poor man, wearing a cloak of brown wool that covered his shoulders. Saint Florentius takes no notice of them. He walks on.

He hobbles through the Great Hall, book in hand.

A sunbeam shines down from an arrow slit to his right. He hangs his cloak on it.

He goes up to Dagobert's throne, kneels, kisses the hem of the Frankish king's robe. He opens his mouth and says:

'I mean to go as far as Niederhaslach.'

Saint Florentius was such a great scholar that he had the power, wherever he might be, of hanging his cloak on sunbeams.

5. The Villa at Épinay in the Snow

Buzzards don't fly, they glide in the air. To be even more precise, they float on the air that bounces back from the surface of the earth.

They can rise very high on thermals. Their yellow beaks and grey feet disappear from view. That is when they are happiest.

You should never look directly at a bird of prey.

They don't come to those who look at them.

You have to turn your gaze elsewhere

and make your arm a dead branch in space.

Then you suddenly receive it,

heavily,

on your glove, and you go into the trees.

Dagobert falls ill in his villa at Épinay in December 638. Feeling death near, he has himself carried on a waggon in the snow as far as the hermitage at Saint-Denis, where, at the commencement of his reign, he built a new chapel.

On the point of expiry, on 19 January 639, the king requests of the abbot that he be buried near Saint Dionysos—beneath his martyr's cloak—near the saint who had protected him in the past, yet not in the choir where that man's bones lay, but in the transept to the right of the altar, on the side the French call *côté cour*.

6. Rotrude

In 781, Charlemagne promises his daughter Rotrude (Rodthruda) to the young *basileus* Constantine (Konstantinos).

Rotrude sets to studying Greek to be prepared for the capital of the Eastern Empire and also in the hope of seeing Leander's tower.

She learns to sing, in the Greek tongue of Byzantium, the poem of the man who leaps into the sea out of love.

It fell to Frater Lucius of the Abbey of Saint-Riquier to teach the Greek language to young Rotrude.

In 787, Irene has the eyes of her son Constantine put out so that she can stay in power. The engagement of Rodthruda to Constantine is broken off.

It was Charlemagne, while still king of the Franks, who offered the bishoprics and indefensible frontiers to the *vassi* (the vassals, the marquis, the counts) and the abbeys, which copied and distributed books, to the *missi* (the bishops, the abbots, the clergy).

Paul the Deacon was actually called Warnefried.

One day in 787, he leaves the service of Charlemagne, who is still king. He is so fat that it is difficult to hoist him up on to a mule. He slowly climbs the steep path up to the monastery of Monte Cassino and retires there for good.

In 789 comes a revolution. Charlemagne, while still king of the Frankish tribes, calls on Paul the Deacon once again. By way of an order issued by Paul, he imposes regular Sunday sermons in the vernacular. Then, through a universal recommendation (*admonitio generalis*) which he assigns Alcuin to draft, the king of the Franks lays down the Gallican style of singing (*cantilena romana*) for the whole territory of the Franks. Lastly, Alcuin, on his own initiative, puts a third provision in place: he orders country priests to create, beside their chapels or near their residences, schools for children who show some aptitude for study.

In 799, as Nithard and Hartnid are preparing to learn to read, write and count in the Abbey of Saint-Riquier, three levels of instruction exist: rural schools in the parishes, cathedral schools in the cities, and libraries of holy and classical manuscripts, both of them copied in the scriptoria of the monasteries.

7. Evil

It was Fredegar who continued Gregory's work, while Einard gave way to Nithard: these were the first four writers who composed the marvellous tales that tell the story of the Franks.

Now, it is true that writing is not about raising one's hand to the sky.

Writing is not in any way about blessing.

Writing is lowering one's hand towards the ground, or the stone, or the lead, or the skin, or the page, and it means noting down evil.

The prophet Isaiah cried out: '*Vae qui scribunt, scribentes enim scribunt nequam*!' (Woe to those who write for, in writing, they write what should not be written!)

Now, this is true. What Isaiah's cry to the Hebrew tribes warns of is right: among people who create, there comes a strange gaze deep within themselves which draws on the depths of their body. That gaze seems to sprout from the depths of their ancient life. In fact, it comes from hell. It originates with the dead, it descends in a direct line from the world of wild beasts, it emerges from days of yore— from time long gone.

This brow that furrows, these eyebrows that knit, this silence that descends, this hand that hovers—all are gathered towards a mysterious unity.

In all the cases envisaged, in the most complete mutism, this ecstasy which doesn't yet have words to express itself, this empty-eyed speculation, this oneiromancy that investigates and searches, this enigma—all are delivered or engendered elsewhere than among the living.

They are turned towards another world than the world.

They have their being in another time than the times in which warriors make war, merchants do their deals, ploughmen plough.

'The writer in the book is the book itself. This is how a strange meaning emanates from it, depending on the particular age and world.'

This is what Einhard said to Carolus Magnus while he was still king of the Franks.

And it is what Nithard repeated to his cousin Charles the Bald.

8. Angilbert's Poem

It so happens that the father of Prince Nithard—who was also the father of his twin brother Hartnid—a man called Angilbert who was canonized a saint, knew the three languages. For the ceremony of his induction, the abbot of the Abbey of Saint-Riquier composed a long poem entitled *Signa Deus bis sex acto lustraverat anno* (For God had fulfilled the course of the year by way of twice six signs). In that long poem made up of five cantos and written in the style of Virgil, Angilbert explained why, according to the Franks, at the end of the solar year the strange stolen time of the wolves emerged. Why was the god of heaven so impenetrable? Why did the sun's outward and return journeys not match up? The year had unforeseeable ecstasies in it. That was what the year obscurely opened up, and the test it posed. The end of the year represented both the distressing state of failing time and the great battle men must unleash to re-establish it. For, according to all the narratives of the Franks, the Black She-Wolf of the Heavens not only devours the moon every month in the course of time: she also eats the twelve months and, one fine day, the dish is bare and everything goes black. 'Oh days when the sun ceases to be light! Oh days when the night threatens to spread forever beneath the vault of the heavens! You, men, you no longer know how to count exactly from the stones, using the shadows they cast, and one day the Old Woman will swallow the world once and for all if you don't take more care! O priest of the dawn . . . abase yourself, kiss the earth, let hang the time that hangs and bleeds in the maw of God!'

But Nithard told his father:

'Father, here is why I think we must do something for Sköll and Hati! They are twins like me, Nithard, and my beloved brother Hartnid. Why don't we sacrifice a man of thirty-three and offer him in our turn to the Twelve?'

The Abbot had Sar the Shaman brought to him. But Sar said:

'You are wrong. The wolves are our brothers. They are much closer to ourselves than you are. They are much closer to ourselves than the two brothers Nithard and Hartnid who look so alike! Oh you, whose names are identical even if the letters have been jumbled, where have we seen you together? Where has Hartnid gone whom I loved and who has begun now to roam the frozen seas of the North, to sail to the East? What is he doing now amid the sands of the Orient and its mirages and mountains and their perpetual snows? When have we seen you conversing together since the end of childhood and the coming of sexual desire divided you? Whereas the howling of wolves when the moon is full is perfectly comprehensible to us. As are the songs of the cockerel and the blackbird at dawn. We do not, as we believe, project our melancholia on to the cries that all animals—whatever kind they may be—address to the full moon in the night sky. From the depths of them, from the depths of their insatiable bellies, the old she-wolf addresses her sadness even to us, who are merely a part of her lamentation. Just as the warriors' genitals are merely a part of the crescent of the moon that is suddenly extinguished in the dark cavern women open to them, with their moist fingers, for them to put it in. The She-Wolf is closer to your heart than the hearts of women ever will be! Oh mothers, into whose entrails you penetrate so that they become as rounded and full as the moon itself that changes shape each evening over the course of the month! Here is what we must say: "From the depth of the bellies of the dogs a long barking reaches to the very depths of our being.

It was dogs that drew us close to them, that taught us life in packs, hunting and the journey the moon makes along the vault between the Bear and the Stag. Songs are always of hunger, dreams, desire! We share the same meat, the same riven experience, the same misalignment of two kingdoms whose gates of horn and ivory do not mesh together when we try to close them at the end of the year or at the end of days. They weep when we weep and wail for the initial cavern which lies behind us like a pursuing darkness—a darkness we shall never fail to reach, even as we try to distance ourselves from it as much as possible, so greatly does it horrify us. We too have mouths full of blackness and fill them each day with dead." '

V

(The Book about the
Sixteenth of the Kalends of March)

1. The Kingdom of the Franks

Once upon a time, one day, a day in 569, what is called the Kingdom of the Franks (*regnum Francorum*) replaced what was called old Gaul (*Gallia transalpina*). The tribes of the Gauls had either been annihilated one by one, or deported and enslaved by the Roman legions. The kings who had authority over the leaders of the Franks never built their palaces in southern Europe. They were too fond of wild animals, dark forests, the shocking, dauntless, torrential song of the falling rain, the dazzling beauty of the snow coming down in silence for months on the plains and lying there, the ears of the does that prick up and the improbable antlers that stack up proudly on the velvety heads of the stags. The oak woods the warriors favoured towered over the fields of spelt, wheat and rye and over the rivers full of pike, blue trout, crayfish and eels. The bears, boars, wolves, the birds of prey—these they made into their stone signs or used to decorate their bronze insignias. They were all hunters even before they were warriors, who are merely hunters of men. Their place is in the dark forest. King Charles is preceded by the four venerers: the master of arms, the master falconer, the master of hounds and the master of horse.

Charlemagne loved two things above all else.

The forests.

His daughter Bertha.

Einhard wrote the description in Latin of Princess Berehta. She and her father Karel were alike as two peas in a pod. The same hair, the same very high-pitched voice, the same mouth, the same thickening of the neck, the same very large, round, keen eyes, the face always open and joyful (*facie laeta, hilari*), the same bulging stomach (*venter projector*). Bertha was Charles if he had been a woman. When Bertha had her twins, to which the Duke of Coastal Francia gave the equally twin names of Nithard and Hartnid, Karel der Grosse refused to let Bertha marry Angilbert. He saw the rivalry between his sons as trouble enough, without adding the cupidity of sons-in-law to the rapacity of daughters-in-law. At Aix-la-Chapelle (Aachen), the King of the Franks lived surrounded by his wives, his concubines and all his daughters. It wasn't exactly a harem, nor was it a court. Einhard writes that it was a *contubernium*: a company of women. It was *une compagnie de femmes*, the way one speaks in French of *une compagnie de sangliers*—a 'company' of boars.

2. The King's Journey into the Alps

Charles-le-Magne spends Christmas 799 at Aix-la-Chapelle where he hunts in his grounds in the snow.

At Easter 800, he is at the Abbey of Saint-Riquier where he celebrates the resurrection of Our Saviour Jesus Christ with Angilbert, Bertha, Nithard and Hartnid. He strips off his clothes and plunges into the wonder-working spring.

At Tours, he is received by Alcuin, who places the holy cloak of Saint Martin on his shoulders: the cloak doesn't burn them. Then the King, whom God has chosen, sets out on the paths of the Alps.

The beauty of Ravenna, encircled by ditches and pines and covered in mosaics, diverts and enchants him.

On 23 December 800, Pope Leo III welcomes Charlemagne and his people (including Bertha and Angilbert) to Nomentum, twelve miles from Rome, maintaining the ancient distance set down by protocol.

It is here that the banners are unfurled. It is here that the 'triumph' properly so-called begins—in Latin, the *adventus Caesaris*. The king of the Franks on horseback, at the head of his lords, arrives in the City as emperor, even before the religious authority crowns him.

Charlemagne immediately convenes a synod in the Basilica of St Peter (*templum Pietri*).

King Charles receives the 'purgatory oath' of Pope Leo III before the—seated—bishops and abbots and the—standing—counts and princes.

As Charlemagne remains seated, the Pope stands, goes up to the ambo and pronounces the oath.

The council begins its deliberations and, employing succinct argumentation, re-establishes the empire: since Byzantium has fallen into the hands of a woman (Irena), the title of emperor (*nomen imperatoris*) is declared vacant.

The two assemblies, the Christian and the Frankish, acclaim him clearly and forcefully. In this way, in the choir of the basilica, *potestas* and *nomen* (sovereignty and title) suddenly come together again.

The *Annals* note drily: 'On 23 December 800 Carolus chose not to reject the request of the bishops and people and accepted the name of emperor' (*suscepit imperii nomen*).

3. The Crowning of the Emperor

On 25 December 800, the coronation ceremony is held in the Vatican basilica.

It precedes the solemn Mass celebrated at the altar dedicated to the apostle Saint Peter.

There are four stages to it.

It begins with the *prosternatio* of Charlemagne in the style of the Byzantines, the full-length prostration of the body on the stone floor (*proskinesis*).

Then the king rises and Pope Leo III carries out Charles' coronation (*Carolus coronatus*).

There follows the *consecratio*, by which the Pope admits the emperor into the order of bishops.

Last comes the *acclamatio* of the Roman citizens, naming 'Charles crowned by God emperor of the Romans' and the plebiscitary cry of the Frankish warriors of 'Life and Victory!'

New coins are struck.

On the obverse they bear the head of Charles wreathed in laurel leaves, surrounded by the Latin inscription *Karolus Imperator*.

The reverse has on it the temple of Saint Peter at Rome surmounted by a cross, which is itself encircled by the inscription in Latin: *Christiana Religio*.

4. The Death of Charlemagne

During winter 813, the emperor Charles-le-Magne is ill. In his fever, he allows himself to die of hunger.

He expires on 28 January 814 at nine in the morning.

The duke of coastal Francia Angilbert follows him immediately into death.

His son Nithard buries his father in the precincts of the abbey church of Saint-Riquier in a leather coffin adorned with enamels.

Hartnid is nowhere to be found.

At Aachen all the wives and concubines and daughters of Charlemagne are driven out of the palace by Louis the Pious.

Bertha, Theotrada, Hiltrude, Gisela and Emmen climb under the canvas cover of a cart in the January cold.

They are all allocated to different convents.

5. Nithard the Historian

In June 840, Louis the Pious dies. Nithard immediately throws in his lot with Charles the Bald, son of Judith Welf of Bavaria and Louis the Pious and the youngest of his second cousins, who has just celebrated his seventeenth year.

In July 840, Charles the Bald sends Count Nithard, accompanied by Adalgar, as his ambassador to Lothair (Ludher), who rejects any agreement with his young brother Charles (Karle) to share the empire between them.

The three legitimated grandsons of Charles-le-Magne cannot agree.

During the winter of 840, Einhard is found dead at the monastery of Seligenstadt.

What Einhard was for Charles-le-Magne, the royal secretary, the writer of his *History*, Nithard becomes for Charles the Bald.

It is in mid-May 841, when they are at Châlons-en-Champagne, that Charles the Bald asks Nithard—both being grandsons of Charlemagne—to write his *Historia*, so as to put an end to the malicious gossip and slander about his reign that is doing the rounds, and also to head off the malicious stories being developed—and already malevolently spread—about the war-to-the-death the three sons of Louis the Pious are preparing to wage.

6. The Battle of Fontenoy

On 21 June 841, the three brothers' three campaigning armies meet between Sens and Auxerre around a swamp beside a wood.

Suddenly, they hesitate.

Lothair decides to head for Saint-Sauveur-en-Puisaye and establishes his army in the heart of the Forest of Fontenoy.

Having formed a pact, the armies of the two younger brothers, Charles and Louis, sweep around him. They install themselves at Thury.

On 25 June 841 at eight in the morning, the Battle of Fontenoy begins, on the edge of the Puisaye forest.

Battle is joined at first light on the brook of the Burgundians (*rivolum Burdigundonum*), known today as the brook of Saint-Bonnet, since, among the Franks proper names have grown shorter, gradually becoming distilled down as the cycles of the seasons have progressed. From the first assault, Charles the Bald (Karle) and Louis the German (Lodwigs) clash extremely violently with Lothair (Ludher). Nithard, the king's secretary, not only watches the whole battle and reports it in his account but also takes part in it under the command of Seneschal Adalhard.

Nithard writes: 'Immense was the booty, immense the slaughter.'

Lothair and the ragged remnants of his army flee, abandoning all waggons.

Sunday 26 June 841 is given over to burying the dead, friends and enemies without distinction, since all of them are Franks.

A council immediately called by Charles the Bald and Louis the German ratifies the victory of their united armies. The bishops and abbots declare: 'The judgement of God almighty (*judicium Dei omnipotentis*) was made clear in the blood of the battle that was waged.'

They decree a three-day fast. On the one hand, this is for the surviving warriors to purify themselves; on the other, it is to appease the anger of the souls of the dead at the incredible quantity of Frankish blood that has been shed in the forest.

7. The Sacraments of Argentaria

In early 841, Nithard and Charles the Bald are in Paris at the Palace of Saint-Cloud.

In his book, for the date of 18 October 841, 6.57 a.m., Nithard notes the marvellous oddity he sees above the tops of the trees in the Bois de Saint-Cloud. It is an eclipse of the sun. On that event, he closes the second book of his *Histories*.

In early February 842, the two armies that were victorious at the Battle of Fontenoy are at Strasbourg in the icy cold, where they set up camp, the one on the banks of the Ill, the other on the banks of the Rhine.

Half-way between them, on the frozen plain, late in the morning of Friday 14 February, the two kings and the chieftains—the leaders of the tribes—solemnly declare an oath of peace between them and, before God, strike a pact of—maleficent, sacred—mutual assistance against Lothair.

It is at this point, in the cold of late morning on Friday 14 February 842, that a strange mist rises from their lips.

They call it French.

Nithard, the first to do so, wrote French.

What we refer to nowadays as the 'Strasbourg Oaths' were called in Latin by the bishops and abbots the 'Sacramenta Argentariae'.

It is Nithard himself who makes clear in his *Historia* that the city of Argentaria on the river Ill is 'now called Strasbourg by most of its inhabitants' (*nunc Strazburg vulgo dicitur*).

Rare are the societies that know the tipping point of the symbolic: the birth date of their language—the circumstances, the place, the weather.

The chance event of an origin.

There is something miraculous in being able to observe the encoding. In being able to contemplate the wild moment of *literal transference*. We can see the confusion generated by the new symbolic reign it suddenly establishes. There is no half-language: a human breath in the cold air *switches* language. We are touching the void here: touching pure contingency. The change from 'Latin' to 'French' is as unforeseeable as the substitution of the word Strazburg for Argentaria is contingent.

8. Strazburger Eide

So stupefying is this fortuitous birth, so much does it define territory, so much does it change the course of time that I am going to be as precise as I can possibly be. On Friday 14 February 842, at the end of the morning, in the cold, we ascended seven flights in a single instant.

Seven stages were passed through which have to be clearly distinguished.

1. The *sacramentum* (*serment*: oath) is prepared by the diocesan bishops and the abbots in Latin (*lingua Latina*).

2. The two kings, when they swear (*juraverunt*), cross languages the way the Greeks of Byzantium do (that is to say, in the manner of two *symbola* pieces that are brought together like terracotta tesserae that have been broken; with the result that the royal proclamations mesh together forever from language to language and from people to people).

3. The German king Louis, being the elder, takes the oath in *French* (*in lingua romana*) before his brother's troops.

4. The French king, Charles the Bold, being the younger, pronounces the oath in *German* (*in lingua teudesca*) before his brother's troops.

5. The leaders—in Latin the *duces* (which gives us English *dukes*)—of the tribes of the German Franks

pronounce before their troops, in their rustic language (*in lingua rustica*—that is to say, in their own language, which in the case of the German tribes is proto-Germanic) the pact to the death that has been struck between the kings, so that all the German-speaking warriors can grasp its meaning.

6. The leaders—in Latin the *duces* (which gives us English *dukes*)—of the tribes of the 'French' Franks pronounce before their troops, in their rustic language (*in lingua rustica*—that is to say, in their own language, which in the case of the French tribes is proto-French) the pact to the death that has been struck between the kings, so that all the French-speaking warriors can grasp its meaning.

7. Lastly, in his book Nithard notes *in the three languages* (Latin, German, French) the oath that was pronounced solemnly in its three 'kinds', when the winter sun was at its zenith on 14 February 842 in the former Argentaria, a town on the banks of the Ill which ever since that day has been called 'Strazburg'.

So, one winter's day, a Friday, French and German found themselves side by side on a plain in Alsace and inside a chronicle which, for its part, is written in Latin with the goosequill of court secretary Nithard, on a carefully depilated and scraped calfskin. It is the trilingual Rosetta Stone of Europe.

Argentariae Sacramenta. Strazburger Eide. Serments de Strasbourg. (Oaths of Strasbourg).

9. *En nulle aide ne serai*
I Shall Not Give Him Any Aid

Nithard makes clear that on the day the kings Louis the German and Charles the Bold and the leaders (dukes) of the Frankish tribes made their pact (*pactum*), snow fell abundantly on the frozen ground (*subsequente gelu nix multa cecidit*).

These are the first French words, pronounced in the cold and snow on their frozen lips on 14 February, understood by Nithard and immediately noted while they still hung on the air:

> *Pro Deo amour et pro christian poblo*
> *et nostro commun salvament*
> *si Lodhuwigs sagrament que son fradre Karlo jurat*
> > *ni je ni nul qui en puissent returnar*
> *en nulle aide, contre Lodhuwigs, ne serai.*

Thus the first French text ends with a sublime double negative, which is a terrible curse of ostracism against betrayal.

En nulle aide ne serai—I shall not give him any aid.

Ni je ni nul—Neither I nor no one.

But there was no betrayal.

The empire was divided into three enormous equal parts. Middle Francia stayed in the hands of Lothair. West Francia went to Charles the Bald. East Francia remained under the domination of Louis the German.

We can already see present-day Europe in this.

And in this strange contingency of origins, in this whitish breath that rises from the lips, in this plentiful (*multa*) snow that falls from the sky, all the wars it has known and the rivalries it still knows are written.

10. Leaving in a Flurry of Snow

The very next day, Saturday 15 February 842, Louis the German goes down the Rhine, reaches Speyer and pitches camp at Worms.

The very next day, Saturday 15 February 842, Charles the Bald enters the forests of the Vosges that are heavy with snow. Goes beyond Hunspach. Leaves Wissembourg. From there, King Charles reaches Saarbrücken and is able to relieve the abbey of Saint Arnoul de Metz, which he does on 24 February.

On Thursday 15 June, the oaths of Friday 14 February are countersigned and sealed with the two rings of the two kings on the Island of Ansilla to the south of Mâcon.

The troops of the two kings, Charles the Bald and Louis the German, are stationed on either side of the Saône, equidistant from each other, just as the island itself is equidistant from the river's banks.

The following year, in the heat of August 843, the oaths sworn in the cold of 14 February 842 at Strasbourg and sealed on the Island of Ansilla on Thursday 15 June 842 end in the territorial share-out of the Treaty of Verdun on the West bank of the Meuse.

But Nithard does not travel to the Civitas Verodunensium (the city of Verdun).

VI

(The Book of the Death of Nithard)

1. The Skittish Withdrawal of Nithard

On 14 December 842, Charles the Bald marries Hirmentrude. Hirmentrude is the daughter of Duke Odo, who rules over the Loire valley. She is the niece of Seneschal Adalhard, under whom Nithard served at the Battle of Fontenoy and who was not of his clan. Nithard knows that the division of property is not going to be favourable to him.

Nithard immediately leaves the court of Charles the Bald while it is wintering at Valenciennes.

He rides through the December snow.

He withdraws from political life with sad, broken-hearted words that are wonderful to translate: 'My anxious (*anxia*) thought, besieged by the discords and rivalries, restlessly seeks a way to escape politics completely. But since destiny has so solidly attached (*junxit*) my fate to all that happens in the two rival camps, I find myself, despite all efforts, constantly storm-tossed: thus I have absolutely no idea where I will land up in life.'

The last dated event in Nithard's *History*, at the end of the fourth and final book, is the lunar eclipse of 19 March 843, occurring deep in the jet-black sky.

2. Nithard's Last Will and Testament

On 19 March 843, the moon being black and total darkness having suddenly invaded the world, Nithard sets down his goose quill, puts away his knife and closes his pot of ink.

He becomes lay abbot of the abbey of Saint-Riquier, as his father had been before him.

Frater Lucius is still alive.

Phenucianus the Fowler is still alive.

Creekevild the Painter is still alive.

Bertha is still alive.

His twin Hartnid is still alive.

From a religious point of view, if we compare it with the piety of his father, who in fact became Saint Angilbert, the personality of Nithard is peculiar. He loves the heavens and God—or rather he loves god as the heavens.

In the same way as Abbot Suger, at a later date and in a strange revolution, will make no distinction between god and light.

Count Abbot Nithard asks the friars of the abbey to bury him, were he to die, in Christian ground but directly beneath the stars.

'May my father Angilbert remain in the abbey church, beneath the cross. As for me, let me stay by the door, beneath the sky.'

3. The Death of Nithard

In the spring of 843, the Norman fleet raids Quentovic on the Canche, crosses the English Channel, lays waste to the port of Hamwic, sails up the Thames, ravages London and returns.

In 844, the Nordmannen—Normans—are back. They sack the new abbeys and 'chapels' of the Franks, together with the old villas and 'basilicas' of the Romans on the banks of the Somme, on the banks of the Canche, on the banks of the Seine, on the banks of the Yonne, on the banks of the Loire, and on the banks of the Garonne.

Nithard dies fighting them.

Death comes to the Count Abbot Nithard (*abbas et comes Nithardus*) by a blow struck to his head with a Norman sword.

His skull is split and he dies instantaneously. His legs give way under him. His body collapses into the waves. The black-backed and herring gulls swoop down on him.

His corpse is pulled out onto dry land, pursued by the screeching, squalling birds of the sky.

He is stripped bare. His body is sprinkled with salt (*sale perfusum*).

The body is dressed in purple cloth.

They place him on a wooden litter fringed with leather (*lecticam ligneam coriatam*).

They take the body on a cart to the Abbey of Saint-Riquier.

They bury him beneath one of the steps leading up to the abbey, in the manner he ordered, so that he, like the Franks of old, would be in direct contact with the stars.

Charles the Bald does not travel to the burial.

It is not known whether Hartnid was present at the funeral.

4. The Tears of Sar

One day long ago, Sar the Sorceress sat down by the sea. She wept. She sang to herself:

'Where is Hartnid who left to follow the sun? That's the question I ask each time the heavenly body that had passed out of my sight rises again and I feel its heat warming my hands.

The children's boats are tied to their tiny round hands by a bunch of brown string that is simply a braid of hemp.

Despite being short, the string that binds them to their toys gets tangled in their clumsy fingers.

With the damp, it gradually grows heavy and sticky.

The disorder of desires, the eagerness of repentance, defiance and cowardice entangle it.

All at once, the impatience they feel to stretch it out and pull again on the vessel

they believe they are guiding on the flowing, rising water,

fails to untangle it.

We die so quickly, so soon, and in such cowardly ways, performing worthless tasks.'

Who was Hartnid? How did Hartnid learn of the death of his brother? Where was Hartnid when the Battle of Fontenoy was being fought? Where was Hartnid when the Franks began to speak French in the fog that cloaked the little valleys and canals of the Ill that are straddled by the little wooden bridges of old Argentaria and new Strazburg? Was he present for the territorial settlement at Ansilla on the Saône? Did he go back to Charles' court at Valenciennes when Nithard took the decision to leave it?

But, more temperately, Sar, the shaman of the Bay of the Somme, sang:

'I have begun to seek his face everywhere, in the same way as he looked for that face he sought, but which did not exist!'

5. Sar and Hartnid

In the Temple of Diana the Huntress at Ephesus, the soul of Hartnid told itself: 'If I had known her, perhaps I would have been horrified and run away.'

Then Hartnid, who was at the gates of Ephesus, at the bottom of the mountain, at the same moment, the same day, the same hour when the fairy woman that sat down as day broke and sang on the seashore and let out her moan, plucked Sar's hairs, which he had preserved one by one, from the comb they had been caught on.

Then he burned them all in Diana's flame, except for one which he tied to his neck.

Did Hartnid love the Blind Old Woman?

Perhaps he loved the Nocturnal One? Diana, the goddess with the stags, the moon in the night sky, in whose temple he burned the hair?

Perhaps he quite simply loved the night itself, more than all men, women, ships, horses, their coats and manes, than sails, than black and blue wings or the jay.

The comb was magnificent. It was made of white ivory. Its eight teeth were set with red and copper-coloured stones affixed to the base of the large ivory tooth. But Hartnid had forgotten the queen of Glendalough, for it was she who had gifted it to him. He had abandoned Alyla in Ireland, as he had forgotten Tullins. He had forgotten Lucilla, who had so foolishly declined the bilberry. He had forgotten Macra who was so slim. He no longer remembered Eudoxia of Byzantium. He had so loved women's hair and their endless plaits, their chignons, their fragrance, the silken tresses in which to plunge his face, the bared nape of the neck or the white collar bone or the crook of the ear where he would yield his sigh as he climaxed.

What did the workmanship, the ivory, the stones, the colours and the value matter?

Hartnid abandoned the comb in the reeds and left it to the mud of the seashore.

He kept a single one of Sar's hairs which he tied around his neck, together with a gold coin on which the face of his grandfather was struck.

'This is how one loves,' said Hartnid.

'This is how one leaves this world,' said Hartnid again.

6. The Story of the Fowler called Phenucianus

Phenucianus always had a crow in his hand. The falconer called Phenucianus was a man of wizardry. It was thanks to the crow family (the black crow, the black and blue jay of the oak trees, the rook with its whitened beak) that he met the beings he wished to. He could not read, but he was learned and even 'wise'—that is to say, a sorcerer.

With Nithard dead, Phenucianus became friends with the aged Lucius.

The fowler put the falcons and the eagles and the goshawks and the merlins and the sparrow hawks in cages for the noblemen. But he was in reality a great master who hid a magical hand beneath the poor pecked, torn leather glove of the fowler.

It was, in reality, souls that he trained, so as to send them one by one to heaven.

And the liveliest souls were the darkest.

And the darkest, hand on heart, were the anthracite-black crows.

7. The Teachings of Phenucianus

Phenucianus knew nothing of letters, but he knew all about birds, by which he sent messages to whomsoever he wished in the world.

To Lucius, who had formed the idea of teaching him his letters, he began gradually to teach the songs of the birds.

He began by teaching him to recognize them, and Frater Lucius wept with joy when he managed to distinguish the songs in the woods; to imagine the plump shapes behind the melodies, to picture the colours or shades of the different plumages behind the frequency of the rhythms.

He found pleasure in putting names to them without seeing the actual phenomena, such being the function of language.

As night was ending, Phenucianus took his arm.

'That is the owl we call the sparrow-owl,' he would explain. That's the owl replying to the robin. The owl singing in the night time on the old woodshed roof. They form a duo that bewitches the soul.

'I prefer observing to understanding,' said Phenucianus.

'You are beginning to read,' replied Frater Lucius.

Phenucianus said to Frater Lucius:

'The barn owl can be recognized by its pure white underbelly. Like a piece of eternal snow still clinging to the black vault of the sky. In the depths of night, these downy feathers grow luminescent; they fascinate like a crescent moon; or startle you suddenly like a bolt of lightning. A long, continuous, piercing cry suddenly turns your stomach like a very long sheet being torn lengthwise, the tearing lasting for an age. The barn owl doesn't repeat this cry, which merely indicates to the other nocturnal messengers the place it has found to sleep and in which it is indicating the peace it wishes to find there, in which it finally falls silent. It falls asleep suddenly, with its cry still echoing, on its church tower or on the stones of the old tower or amid the tiles of the ruined roof of the wood store by the river bank. It does this as the pale light of day returns, terrifying it as its only god.

Like the patrician Roman women of old, it never looks at anything square on.

To fight, it tips itself backwards. It doesn't eye its prey, which it merely hears moving about in the darkness, but arches back its head and simply thrusts out its claws like hands to grasp the sound that prey makes.'

'The song it sends out to you, take it as your personal shroud being ripped open.'

'The soul, at just the moment when it tears apart, is thought,' says Frater Lucius.

'I prefer thinking to judging. To experience things is to close one's eyes,' said Phenucianus.

'But in thinking you continue to dream. Thinking, you continue to remain in darkness,' replied Frater Lucius.

Phenucianus said to Frater Lucius: 'Among woodpeckers, the male likes to drum on tree trunks. The woodpecker is the first musician who preferred an instrument to the voice. He might even be said to be his own instrument-maker. His song is that wood which he loves, the wood that is resonant because he hollows it out. A fine instrument-maker who shakes his little scarlet bonnet and scoops out his song anew each day. In this way, he deepens the nests he sculpts and crafts them by ear. He revels in the larvae that the resonance points out to him within the bark. Woodpeckers adore trees and protect them from the larvae they enjoy. They stun these before eating them.'

'I prefer feeling to perceiving,' said Phenucianus.

'It is possible you are preparing yourself to love,' replied Lucius.

Phenucianus said to Frater Lucius:

'Buzzards neither sing nor drum; here's what people say: they mew. Others say—more rarely—that buzzards "whine" rather than mewing. But everything depends on the buzzard. Anyway, it is suddenly like a little cat crying out, clinging to its branch.'

Then Frater Lucius wept, for he remembered a cat he had loved.

Sar the Shaman pushed away the fowler who did not understand the tears flowing down the friar's nose.

The blind old fairy woman went over to Frater Lucius and grasped him firmly. She hugged him to her without saying a word.

He wept and wept.

Then, with the two aged men—though so much less aged than herself—she spoke of Hartnid:

'There are human beings whom their shame—taking on the distress of their ever-slenderer bodies, bodies not so much elevated as hollowed-out, not so much battle-hardened as wounded, abdicating all power and, indeed, coming to terms with disfavour—cloaks in a sort of nobility that eludes our grasp. They are dressed in black and slip into the shadows.'

8. The Adventures of Love

Here is how Hartnid learnt of the death of his grandfather.

He was in the mountains above the port of Ragusa. He was walking in splendid surroundings, thinking of nothing in particular. As he went along his path of box bushes and violets, he felt inexplicably moved.

He thought he could hear a bustard on a branch.

The call that bustards make is a cracking sound.

They crack like the black pods of the broom plant when they open at the time of greatest heat.

Straight away, he knew and boarded a boat.

The death of Angilbert followed immediately on the death of Charlemagne. Thus do friends die.

After first praying with her, he left his mother Bertha.

He didn't see his brother Nithard when he knelt before his father's tomb in the middle of the nave of the abbey church dedicated to King Richarius.

Here is how Hartnid learnt of the death of his brother Nithard.

'Was mir *die Tiere im Wald* erzählen?' asked Berehta in her native tongue of Hartnid when he came back to the convent she had been sent to by Louis the Pious on the death of her father Charles-le-Magne in January 814.

Hartnid, who was behind the grille of the visiting room, had no answer to give his mother.

He already no longer understood the language she was using.

'Ce sont les ruines' Bertha said to him in French. 'What do the *animals of the forest* tell me? They tell me of ruins,' she repeated.

'Was mir die Liebe erzählt?' That is what Hartnid was thinking if we now have to translate his life into Germanic language. He went off again. No one could say in what direction he left. No one knew what he lived on. He travelled. He sailed. He rode. He couldn't keep still. They said that a fairy woman living on the banks of the Somme had saved him when he was a small child. He barely spoke.

He didn't eat. His name was simply the opposite of a name and he was, then, completely indifferent to the world, which was merely the ghost of a world. But here is what his twin brother Nithard thought of him while he still lived. At play here was the indifference of a man whose mind had turned staunchly away from the normal. Something that had the face of a singular woman drew him towards it, tugged at his desires, haunted the hours of his days, appeared in his dreams. He preferred shame to sin, desire to sexual climax, curiosity to kingship, wandering to glory, the ocean and the forest and the animals and the birds to the fortified bridges, the paved alleyways, the town squares, the quaysides, the palace halls and the names of the powerful that are acclaimed there.

Outwardly, he led the life of a saint, but that was mere outward appearance.

Their grandfather had become emperor when they had just barely been born.

Their grandfather had become a dead man after they had gone their separate ways.

His body had been mummified in the crypt beneath the Palatine Chapel.

His heart and his liver had been laid in a strange tomb.

It was a magnificent Roman sarcophagus representing Proserpina, the goddess of the Underworld, at the very moment when, picking flowers on the plain of Enna, she is carried off by the god Hades.

It was the emperor in person who chose this extraordinary goddess of the dead at Ravenna on the edge of the marshes.

He had touched the underside of her beautiful marble face with his hand, with the same gesture that the hermit king of the Saint Marcoul spring made to cure the throats of the Franks.

But for his part, Hartnid, his grandson, unhesitatingly preferred the unknown face of the woman he loved to the Queen of Death.

He even preferred the sweetness of that face to the cross on which God howled with pain, screwing up his mouth.

Prince Hartnid said: 'I don't know why we have formed the habit of calling the following things sinful: marshes, stagnant waters, obsessive, stable, silted-up, repetitive or slow things, shifting sands, contemplations, ecstasies. I don't know why we have formed the habit of calling the following things virtuous: bad weather, death, war, victory, the lightning that strikes, the cry of abandonment, the spear, the sword, the sponge, history.'

9. Hartnid at Baghdad

When he reached Baghdad, Hartnid saw the face at last. And he became convinced that the face of the woman concerned more than resembled the one he carried in his heart. His whole body flushed crimson. He asked after the young woman, who lived in the al-Karkh area of the city, where most of the merchants resided. Then he paid through the nose to rent the house opposite. He furnished it with great care and attention. He had the fountains restored. He had the layout of the garden changed, embellishing it with flowering bushes, orange trees, raspberry bushes, lemon trees, palms and birds.

From the garden, he could see her window.

For six days he was blissfully happy.

When she came to her window to see how the work he was having done in his garden was coming on, he thought to himself: 'That is her face!'

When, hidden in a grove of trees, he looked up at her, what he felt for her was inexpressible.

There are no finer moments to be had in this world than when one catches sight of those one loves, their appearance enhanced by an unexpected resplendence.

He got her to attend, with her father, a feast that he organized with the local leader to honour his neighbours and show off his brand-new home. He greeted her on that occasion and, approaching, said:

'Your hands are red.'

'I spend my days making amphoras.'

'You do not have the face I am looking for.'

'I have my face.'

'You do not have the face I am looking for,' he repeated, greatly vexed.

'This is the face God gave me. I cannot make another with my two red hands.'

10. Juneyd the Sufi

Juneyd the Sufi wrote in 880: 'When it appears, the ground of Being doesn't say: "It is I". The ground of Being knows no I. It appears. Then it closes up again.'

VII

(The Sequence of Saint Eulalia)

1. *In figure de colomb volat al ciel*

Her robe was made from the crystallization of breath that occurs when one breathes out into cold air. You could see everything of her body, from the tips of her breasts stiffened by desire to the outline of her sex, as delicately shaped as an ear.

Her sex simply resembled the letter *e*.

That was the only difference between them.

She had her neck severed: a bird flew out.

2. The Birth of French Literature

The first written trace of the French language dates from Friday 14 February 842 at Strasbourg on the banks of the Rhine.

The first work of French literature dates from Wednesday 12 February 881 at Valenciennes on the banks of the Escaut.

The tradition has given this first poem written in French the title *Sequence of Saint Eulalia*. The canticle, on the page of vellum, is bereft of a title. Why *Sequentia*—Sequence? Because that is the name the priests gave in Latin to the hymns that were sung in the old Roman basilicas, under their ancient domes, and in the new Romanesque temples of the Franks, directly beneath the spectacular vaults of the brand new 'chapels'.

Late in 877, on 6 October, the last Carolingian emperor Charles the Bald—whose secretary Nithard had once been in the 840s—died, wretchedly, in a cowshed in the Maurienne valley, without even the breath of a donkey or ox to warm his limbs and quell his fears.

Early in 878, over a period of eight days, the relics of Saint Eulalia were taken by boat to the inland port of Valenciennes.

On 12 February, the bishop received them there.

That same day, the Latin canticle—the *Sequentia Sanctae Eulaliae*—went up from the mouths of the choir of monks. And in a grand procession, with much singing, all the priests and clergy of the diocese of Valenciennes, followed by the faithful and the slaves of the manses, went to lay the bones of Saint Eulalia in the crypt beneath the main chapel of the Abbey of Saint-Amand.

Three years later, on Wednesday 12 February 881 to be very precise, as part of the preparations for the Procession and annual feast of Saint Eulalia, the Latin cantilena that had been dedicated to Sancta Eulalia was translated into French (*in lingua romana*), so that all the faithful who were part of the cortege and who were following the reliquary containing the bones of the holy martyr of Barcelona, could sing it without having any difficulty grasping the meaning of their song.

The text of this first French poem was set down in Carolingian script, together with its melody, at the end of a manuscript bound in unscraped deer hide.

Hence the name of the manuscript, the *Liber Pilosus* (the hairy book).

It wasn't until 1837, in Valenciennes library, that a scholar noticed these twenty-nine lines of French poetry that had been copied out early in the month of February 881 at the end of the compilation, on the obverse of its closing page of bare deerskin.

The *Liber Pilosus* still exists.

The book is still in Valenciennes library.

If one brings one's spectacles up to the undepilated hide—and one's nose and eyes with them—this old ninth-century bearded book still smells strongly of the Ardennes forest and the black blood of the winter hunt.

French literature begins with a very brief life that runs for twenty-nine lines.

It turns out that the first French soul is a bird and the first line of French verse is decasyllabic.

3. Life of Saint Eulalia

Here is that first line:

Buona pulcella fut Eulalia.

One day long ago, 276 years after the birth of Jesus, in the city of Barcelona under the Roman domination of Diocletian, Eulalia was born.

In 289, during the persecution the Roman Senate had demanded from Diocletian Iovius, the girl—*la buona pulcella*—was jailed in the fortress of Mons Jovicus for being anti-Roman, anti-Jupiterian, anti-sacrificial, in short, Jewish and Christian.

When she had reached the age of fourteen and womanhood, her trial took place before the municipal authorities, in full public view, in the year 290, at the top of the hill that overlooks Barcelona.

The young virgin refused to renounce her error.

Then Maximianus tied her hands together with a rope, made her crawl slowly on her knees down the city's main thoroughfare, from the sea shore to the amphitheatre.

Still on her knees, she ascends the wooden steps leading up to the pyre that has been built.

A Roman centurion sets fire to the branches that send the logs up in flames. Her clothes burn but her flesh does not. It does not even sizzle. Her young girl's spindly, hairless body can be seen naked and intact in the fire: the flames shun her skin.

'Then Maximianus gave the order to behead Eulalia.'

At the moment her head fell, her soul suddenly exited from her neck in the form of a bird.

The first poem in our French language ends with a sublime line. Here is that last line of the first poem to be written in our language:

In figure de colombe volat al ciel [In the form of a dove, she flew to heaven]

French comes out of Latin the way a child comes out of the mother's womb: the way a bird comes out of the saint's neck.

In figure de colombe volat al ciel.

Winter in Latin is a feminine noun.

In the kingdom of the Catalans, Eulalia refers to the old *Hiems* [winter] whose neck is severed at the end of the year. Then, after a long procession made twelve times around the walls of the city and the parish bounds, its straw effigy is burned beside the sea.

Winter is *dead*.

In the night sky there rises the first moon of the lunar year.

The bad days are gone!

The interminable long nights are over.

From the severed head of the old Hiems, spring rises up in the song of the birds.

In the Catalan language: *dans le cant dell ocells*.

The bones of the young martyr are honoured and her fine trisyllabic name is sung on 12 February, in the last frosts and ice, in the pale sunshine that struggles to emerge from the waves of the sea that stretches out below the glorious port of the Catalans.

Eu-lalia in the language of the ancient Greeks means *Fine word*.

The 'fine word' comes out of dead Latin.

The 'fine word' that gives a name in Greek to French comes out of the ancient world the way a bird comes chirping out of the eggshell it breaks, at the end of winter, on the shores of time.

4. The Saint-Riquier Abbey Fire

The *Sequentia Sanctae Eulaliae*—translated into French by a monk using a goosequill on unscraped deer hide—becomes, on Wednesday 12 February 881 at the Abbey of Saint-Amand, the *Cantilena of Saint Eulalia*.

Some days pass.

They are just a few days in that 'storm' that defines the heart of time.

At the end of the month of February 881, the Abbey of Saint-Riquier is sacked by the Norse sailors who are also merciless warriors.

More than a hundred of the three hundred monks that Angilbert had gathered are put to death. The library is partly burnt but, by dint of their thickness, not all the skins are consumed. The black beams smoke above the books, which are as yet untouched by the flames. The stones that were part of the oldest buildings, dating from the sixth century, turn to rubble, collapsing on to the Source aux Puissances that is dedicated to Saint Marcoul. But it was on this day of late February 881 that the autograph manuscript of Nithard's *Historia*, which he had placed there, was lost, just as Heraclitus had put his book *On Nature* into the hands of the stag-headed priests of Diana in the temple of Ephesus. The only copies that remained were those made in the scriptorium of the monastery of Reims at the request of Hincmar, bishop of the diocese of Reims and successor to Nithard.

It is a kind of blackness.

The first book in which our language was written is our language's first burned book.

For Nithard always feared the *Wolfzeit*, and that is why the four very fine books he wrote, dreading the ravages of time, were rooted, in their conception, in solar eclipses.

5. The Two-Castled Ship

A two-castled ship, with a large brown hull and a keel, was able to sail beyond sight of the coasts of Saint-Riquier and navigate the ocean following the stars.

One night, Pope Clement VI had a dream.

When he awoke, he asked to be buried in the pelt of a stag. His request was carried out as soon as he expired, in 1352, so keen was he not to linger in this world. So eager was he, he said, 'to flee the century and his people as fast as he could.'

6. Story of the Child called Le Limeil

One day long ago, when Frater Lucius had grown old, he took on a novice who helped him with his daily tasks. The child was six years old and had a taste for music. He played tunes on his reed pipe with genuine grace. On it he imitated the songs of the birds that the monk taught him in the garden of his cell. He modulated around the segmentation of their songs. All the birds responded to his calls; they let themselves be charmed by his skill; they came to play at his feet; they came to peck around his sandals at the remains of his meals.

The child had an extraordinary ear and it was an old blackbird that taught him the art of modulating by varying the key. Old Frater Lucius taught him the notes, using the Saint-Riquier Tonary to help him set them down on the page. Phenucianus passed on to him the most complex of the songs he had kept in his memory.

The child, who was called Limulus—though the youngest friars preferred to say Le Limeil—was entirely devoted to Frater Lucius. He prepared his meals. He cleaned the floor of his cell. He did his washing. He went to fetch his soup and bread from the refectory.

And, when Easter came around, he even scoured the great wayside cross that had been sculpted atop the stone that stood in the middle of the courtyard lawn using an iron chisel.

Phenucianus, who was skilled with his hands, made a splendid flute for him from dark wood, affixing to it an ivory mouthpiece that had been deftly worked in exactly the style of a blackbird's beak.

It was an incomparable experience to hear him repeat the songs of the birds that throng the skies.

One February night, Frater Lucius got up to go to Matins. He found the child dead in the bed by his side, cold beneath the blanket. He tried to wake him.

To no avail. He was white and dead.

The unhappy Frater Lucius went down the stairs from his cell to get to the service. In the kitchen of his cell, he found on the table the black flute the child had left there. He put it away in the chest.

When Easter came, Frater Lucius went to the stone cross to pray. On the granite pedestal, he saw a blackbird, with a whitish beak, cleaning the stone. He was moved to tears. Pressing back his tears, he said:

'It's very noble of you, little blackbird, to do all this cleaning that Le Limeil used to do!'

'Take a good look to see if I am in fact a blackbird or whether I am, as you say, a little boy, Brother Lucius!'

At first Frater Lucius thought it was the child Limulus, nicknamed Le Limeil, who had come back, but looking closely at the bird, he noticed the white marks on its beak. He came up closer, took it in his hand, looked it in the eye and fell to his knees with the little jet-black bird quivering in his palm: he recognized his dead kitten. His black kitten had come back and turned into a blackbird. Only, the flat black and white mouth of the kitten had become an elongated beak with the same pattern on it; a little less white perhaps, a little more yellow perhaps—at least the marks were the colour of ivory. The blackbird brought back canticles, cantilenas or refrains of incredible beauty. Sometimes Brother Lucius was so captivated by the tenderness and subtlety of its singing that he didn't even hear Hugues in the distance ringing the monastery-tower bell to call him to supper.

7. The Blackbird Spring

When Hartnid had returned from his travels, Frater Lucius said to him: 'Do you know, things are so strange. The little black cat I loved, whose face your father had wiped from my wall, came back in the form of a young blackbird. Its beak isn't yellow as blackbirds' beaks normally are. It's an entirely black bird, as all male blackbirds are, but it has a curious beak with whitish spots. Yet it chirrups as only blackbirds can. It also modulates as it sings, like a little novice I loved, who played his song on the flute, and who was known in the monastery as Le Limeil. It sings marvellous things which recall memories that make my heart shudder to hear them.'

Every year, on the eve of the Triduum of the Passion. Frater Lucius would go over to the courtyard cross, kneel down, put his hands together and watch the blackbird cleaning it.

With the tip of its beak, it removed the dust.

It tore out the moss bit by bit and the little lichens that had wormed their way into the creases in the stone.

The blackbird was patiently rejuvenating the face of God.

When the blackbird died, the residents of the village and of the hamlets around the Abbey of Saint-Riquier, the fishermen who came from the reed-beds, the sailors who came up from the port, the peasants and even the serfs who worked at the windmills, in the mines, in the forges, in the malt-houses, at the cider presses, at the mint, making bricks or building walls, carried on coming to the cross and, taking turns, took the place of the bird to scrub the face of the Christ.

By dint of this work on its upkeep, the statue of the spread-eagled God had grown smooth and shiny as a slab of marble above the spring.

8. Crustacean Lichens

Crustacean lichens love the rocks that are scorched by the blazing sun. They are not exactly mosses. Nor are they mere dust. Somewhere between moss and dust, they coat the dried-out skulls of the carcasses of dead animals—or warriors—abandoned in the desert.

They particularly like to coat the tombstones of the saints the Romans had put to death by torturing them in their arenas or having them publicly devoured by wild animals at the great spring festivals dedicated to Bacchus— also known as Dionysos among the Greeks or Denis at Lutetia.

Golden lichen clings tightly to the polished stones atop the wayside crosses of Ireland, Brittany and also Picardy, those crosses on which the Lord was painfully put to death like a serf, his side pierced by a spear, like a wild boar.

They love the head of God, which they lick or devour.

They love to surround the stone arch that supports the pulley and rope of the iron bucket.

Life gives everyone the role that is beyond him, the role in which we cannot even manage to die.

The thousands of species of lichen are the product of an association—a confraternity, even—brokered between a seaweed and a fungus. It isn't sexual congress or a marriage pact. It isn't old Philemon and Saint Baucis of Phrygia embracing eternally the way ivy and a vine might entwine on a trellis. It is a more circumspect symbiosis, in which the two organisms do not fuse with each other. The sexual pleasures of the two entities I refer to (seaweed and fungus, long-ago and now, green and red, ocean and light) like to remain solitary, their joys the more certain for their perfect grasp of the course of them, their modes of being profiting from remaining rigorously distinct. Only in the meals between them is there a sharing, those meals giving rise to a kind of dialogue, a sort of joy, contact or exchange. The seaweed feeds the fungus, which absorbs the water and gives it back, while the seaweed carefully filters the sun's rays that it absorbs. They grow with infinite slowness. They advance by one millimetre a year. The staging-posts that desire offers for their waiting are a delight. Their lives, which are almost infinite existences, are counted in millennia, unlike humans on earth or singing children or horrendously murdered black kittens or mayflies that fall dead on the water in a single morning. They help us measure the ancient times that humans find troubling, times that reach back to an incognizable age when they did not exist on earth. Hares nibble at them and reindeer graze on them. Birds use them to build their nests. Lichens form heathlands across which little snails advance, snails that are so many little Frankish knights, with their curling, brownish caparisons, that have invaded this world and became shrunken. The sea is born from their slime.

9. The Peziza on Black, Dead Wood

Suddenly they call: 'Halt!'

They drop the reins, as only snails can do amid the moss and blueberries.

They rest beneath the wonderful red cups of the peziza fungus, which spring up like parasols on the dead black wood.

VIII

(The Book of Eden)

1. Eve's Garden

Already, long ago, there had been a dialogue beneath a tree. It was reported in the oldest of books. That was in Paradise. Eve pointed to a mouth-watering, brightly coloured, round fruit hanging on the end of a branch. A serpent spoke to her. She grabbed the fruit and it filled her palm. It was winter. Such is the history of the world.

Now here is the beginning of our story.

There was a mountain covered with eternal snow. There was a pine tree. There was a dead horse, a sword that nothing breaks, a horn that doesn't sound.

A man alone who dies in the mountains.

2. The Isle of Oissel

The sailors who came from the North and built the frightening vessels known as *knarrs* or *drakkars* adored the valleys of the Somme and the Yonne.

Ragnar Lodbrok said: 'The men who live there are Franks. They are fearful, cowardly, drunken, generous. The buildings of Saint-Riquier and Saint-Germain are brimming with gold. The Isle of Oissel, in the Seine near Rouen, may well be paradise.'

In 858, the Norsemen or Normans captured the royal basilica dedicated to Saint Denis, taking the abbot hostage. His name was Louis, he was Nithard's half-brother and arch-chancellor to Charles the Bald. The ransom paid to the Viking chieftain was 688 pounds of gold and 3,250 pounds of silver.

In 886, Charles the Fat gave 700 pounds of silver to the Normans to have them skirt around Paris and pillage Sens and Vézelay rather than Lutetia and the old palace ramparted long ago by the Emperor Julian.

In 911, at Saint-Clair on the banks of the Epte, Charles the Simple gave Rollo (Hrolfr) his daughter's hand in marriage. He ceded the whole of the land along the coast to him, from Belgic Gaul to the border of the province of Brittany. This long stretch of sea and land, so rich and beautiful, then cast off the name of coastal Francia over which Angilbert once reigned, and became known as the land of the Normans, or Normandy.

3. The Sea

At Quend, in the distance, near the vessels of the Nordmannen, who have dropped their anchors into the silted-up sea floor, far out from the mouth of the estuary— further out than the flat round boats of the Saxons and Irish—the waves roll in as night falls and the wind gradually drops in the darkness. If you move away from the port, if you leave the re-dredged inlets and the *habers* behind you, if you get out of sight of the landing stages, if you move into the reed beds, between the clumps of reeds and the birds that gather and hide there in the marshes, either to hide one's wealth or to pleasure oneself in one's fingers, one glimpses the whitened crests of spume rising up in the still rather bespattered darkness above the shining surface of the sea.

They make a noise that seems ever more enormous in the calm of evening.

It isn't known to whom this enormous noise is directed, this noise the water makes as it intrudes upon the earth— which raised itself up above it, so long ago, driven by the force of fire—and at which it goes on endlessly gnawing.

It isn't known what may be meant by this cry that the sea hurls infinitely into space to nothing visible, doing so so long before ears existed, so long before life itself was born on the planet in the depths of the different enigmatic oceans of the single—if not homogeneous—sea that girds it.

Does the moon attract the sea which rises towards it and growls at its faint light?

Why were there so many sounds before auricles began to appear along the sides of faces, before they were scooped out and opened?

Who knows the meaning of this return of the sea towards the earth—in which what moves outward bends in on itself, in which what advances does so by rolling itself up; which nothing ever appeases and which is never done with being reborn and weeping—a return that has no end we can possibly imagine?

Sar improvised this poem:

> O sound that roars,
> even more inexplicable than the—oh so dark—
>   heavenly night at the heart of the stars,
> sound that deafens the hearing to the point of
>   hollowing out the stomach and filling it with
>   anxiety when we attend to it for more than
>   an hour,
> one's feet in its spume, one's behind soaking on
>   its sands,
> sound that thickens the inner black night, like an
>   astringent salt or a perforating acid,
> that grabs one's head and seizes the heart as soon
>   as one's ears yield to it and are captivated by it,

resonating in the—oh so gloomy—inside of the
skull, where the viscous, delectable brain of
humans involutes,

sound that even engulfs a part of ourselves in the
shells that are broken at the end of the flow
that drives them back to shore,

which beats it and pushes it back into the soft,
springy seaweed so that it twists and tangles
together, before unravelling,

brown, like long sticky sexes, soaking in their
own seed,

black with the blackness that squid shoot out in
order to survive deep in the abyss by making
themselves invisible to the threatening,
approaching, longing eyes.

O sound that roars, that scolds endlessly like a
mother,

and leaves you motionless, almost weak,

and, at times, even overflowing with sadness!

We squat down irresistibly before you.

The bones of our knees touch the wet grains of
sand and sink into them.

We lower our noses directly before the little crests
of the spume.

Our noses and faces end up soaked with drops of
dew and white salt,

our hearts genuinely trembling beneath the whitish
    arcs formed by the ribs,
beneath the two browner little tips of the breasts
    that the cold has raised from the skin,
fearful in our cries, barely existent, uncertain, right
    at the ocean's edge,
humbled beneath the wind,
crumpled beneath the weight of the din of the
    presence of the raging sea,
as if deaf to its howling cry.

The cleft of the buttocks is frozen, the anus retracts,
    your heels have sunk into the sand and your
    toes are full of it,
your mind tiny, compressed, oppressed,
alone as a Prefect of Brittany on his mountain in
    his snow,
lacking firmness,
the upper body prostrate before the little rolls of
    old waves which swell and come closer,
which pull back again almost before they have
    arrived,
which return even larger, even fiercer, spitting even
    more curses,
their shark blues suddenly standing out against
    crow blacks
just as the flight feathers of jays do at the very tip
    of their dark feathers.

4. *Li val tenebrus*

My brothers, the sun is dying out.

The sun that lights the cities and our faces, that lights horses, ships, ports and seas is nearing its end.

It has shone longer over nature than it will in future over the mountains and continents that form the earth's crust.

The system it once produced is already coming apart.

Life that chance made possible here is beginning to perish and the great civilizations are doing their utmost to destroy it,

with the means at their disposal,

which they are adapting,

combining,

multiplying.

There will no longer be anything with any notion of what the sea was,

what life was,

what nature was,

what animals were.

But listen!

Listen in the silence of twilight!

In the most absolute silence, lend your ears.

The planet men call Earth emits a hum that is to this day unexplained.

Totally black waves underlie this barely audible, very low-frequency song that never ends.

The toing-and-froing of the sea across the sloping plateaus of the deep sea floor,

at the point when it reverberates against the shores of the continents,

sings.

5. The Disappearance of Brother Lucius

We do not know how Frater Lucius met his end. He disappeared. In the daybook of the abbey church of Saint-Riquier, it is written that Brother Lucius was lost in the forest. Was he eaten by a wild beast? Gored by a she-bear? Did he have his throat torn out by a wolf? Had he become so averse to the duke of coastal Francia called Angilbert that he ran away—or was he pursued by his ghost? One of the last things recorded of him is a statement reported by an old bird-catcher whom, at the end of his days, he taught in his cell to read and write: 'At the end of his life, Frater Lucius had concluded that all humans who did not like cats had, without exception, an aversion to freedom.'

6. The *Lambeau des Mères*

To the south of the Ballon d'Alsace and Mont Terrible, that is to say, above the virgin forests of the Ardennes, lived a woman with the gift of second sight called Sar.

She was born of Usseloduna in the time of Rome, who was also called la Loubiée. And she too claimed to go back to the most ancient crypts and caves and springs and gorges of the cliffs.

Neither ever left the place where she was born.

Perhaps La Loubiée may even have been Sar.

They say she was loved by Hartnid when he was very young, even though she was much older than him. But what does age matter in the face of desire? He found infinite joy in her slit, but she lost her eyes.

The fairy woman Sar had the gift of prophecy. She was always extremely clairvoyant. She said: 'In the inner corner of our eyes, we have a tiny pink fragment like crumpled skin. Who knows why the Origin has pushed it into the corner of the eye? And who knows, even, why it squashed it up somewhat when it confined it there? I shall tell you the reason for this little bit of pink skin in the corner of men's and women's eyes. This has to do with the Father of the Origin itself, the sun-bearing god Karasu who reigns over the blackness of the depths of night. This little bit of pink flesh is the vestige of the second, translucent, milky eyelids which birds were equipped with before human beings emerged.'

This second eyelid was that of dreams.

Its role was to sweep the eyeball clean and humidify it in its effort to see, in order to enhance their desire to grasp.

Among the sons of the Great Crow—that is to say, among Men—it has shrunk back to form this little foreskin of pink flesh that still persists by the side of their gaze, as it does at the base of their childhood bellies, in such a way as to shield their source.

Tears well up there.

The old men of ancient times, who derived from the birds, called it the *lambeau des mères*—the 'mothers' flap'.

'*Nictat*' the Seer of the *lambeau des mères* said of him— 'He blinks'.

'He devours more than he forgives.'

'He consents.'

'He weeps perhaps more than he climaxes.'

'Can we distinguish between climaxing and weeping?'

'He weeps over Nithard, whom his twin brother had not seen for so many seasons when he had his skull cleft by a sword and fell head first into the waves of the Atlantic!'

7. Hartnid Hearing the Laughter of the Dead

In late 877, Hartnid, having passed the age of seventy-nine years on the first day of October, which is sacred to Saint Remigius—when the last Frankish emperor, Charles the Bold, had breathed his last breath in a poor shepherd's hut that didn't even have windows—and feeling that he too was close to death, called his family and friends to his bedside. He told them:

'I'm dying.'

'We're aware of that,' they replied.

'Why do you say that?'

'It shows on your face, Hartnid.'

'No, it shows quite simply in my age. I shall soon be eighty years old and I'm completely bald!'

'There, you're wrong, Hartnid! It isn't your advanced age that's at issue. Nor is it the hair you've lost that foretells your imminent death! It can be seen in the features of your face.'

'It's just thirty-three years now since my little twin brother Nithard died.'

'Indeed, he died in the bay. We pulled him out of the water, pickled his body, carried him on the planks of a cart, laid him beneath a stone slab and he rests now in the first sarcophagus that was granted to your father, covered simply with his red stole, directly beneath the stars. But, there again, it isn't the commemoration of the death of your younger brother Nithard, the first-born, that drives your lips into the inside of your mouth and explains our seeing clearly that you are dying.'

Then Hartnid lowered his head and made no reply.

'It's your eyes, Hartnid, which say that you are dead! Look how hollow your eyes are. Do you want us to bring you a mirror so you can see them?'

He shook his head. Then Hartnid mumbled: 'No, I don't need you to bring me a mirror to have my death brought home to me. It's true that my body is almost empty. But it's true, too, that my soul is in torment.'

'Then stop inflicting pain on yourself. It isn't normal for death to so torment a man who already has one foot in the next world.'

'You really don't understand anything about anything!' he replied vehemently. 'It's clear you can't grasp what's happening. It isn't the fact that I'm dying that's tormenting me.'

'Then tell us more precisely what's worrying you so much and perhaps we can bring you the help you are crying out for.'

'What's tormenting me is difficult to express, as it comes from the world of the dead and not from me.'

'So it has to do with the death you feel deep within you.'

'No, this isn't about *my* death, but the dead I have to meet again. The dead who are already dead. It's about people long dead who are speaking to me.'

'Nithard?'

'No it isn't Nithard speaking to me from the depths of the world of the dead. My brother has never given me pain. My brother was always there with me. From before my birth, he was there with me! He protected me. He loved me. I ran from him so much because all that love of his was stifling!'

'What's troubling you then?'

'There are dead people I know well at my heels and dead people I like less pricking at me. The former are on my heels like the night "mare". It's a sound of horses' hooves ringing out behind me, pursuing me wherever I go. The second prick at me the way a gadfly stings animals by day. Like a fly buzzing around my face, rootling in the hair of my beard, constantly trying to sting me round the eyes or to get into my nostrils.'

Hartnid and Nithard's two nieces burst out laughing.

Then they sat down on the bed where Hartnid was dying.

He went on: 'These two kinds of dead people are questioning me and I don't know how to reply. Why was I not alongside my brother Nithard in the fighting on the Somme? Why didn't I go and fight under Seneschal Adalhard in the forest of Fontenoy? Why did I never go to Rome like my grandfather Charles-le-Magne to see the sheep grazing in the ruins amid the blue olive trees on the seven hills of the ancients? Why did I never strut down the Via Flaminia? Why didn't I pay my respects to the Ara Pacis? The dead won't stop asking why, why, why.'

'You don't see that the dead are mocking you, Hartnid! These reproaches that they are sending you belong to a different time! Of course you're not the Emperor Charlemagne! You're the grandson he failed to acknowledge, to whom he showed affection only out of respect for your mother, and you outlived Louis the Pious! You loved Emmen, his daughter's daughter! There's no need to be tormented by what the dead tell you.'

'But you haven't got it at all! What they might do to my good name is of no concern! But they are *dead*—and that's what tortures me: I alone—I Hartnid—*remember* them. I alone have access to their memory. I see them again. I see their faces. I'm the only one now who knows their faces. I can even still see how they held themselves. I see again the movements of their hands, the way they sat up or arched their necks when they listened to me. And then, all

154

of a sudden, they turn and look at me for no real reason. They don't understand what I'm doing. They stare wide-eyed and ask why I'm not with them. Why I'm not by their sides in death. What am I doing so far from them? Why am I lingering on among the living?'

'But you loved them, Hartnid! You haven't forgotten them! You haven't betrayed them! You've slept with so many women who were so big-hearted and beautiful and you've not made them unhappier than they were. It's envy, impatience, anger that make them speak this way, to belittle your joys one by one.'

'My friends, I'm not simple-minded. I know the shades of the dead are mocking me. I can see from their faces the dirty trick they're playing on me. So I'm not trying to define what's causing my distress.'

'What torments you then, Hartnid?'

'What pains me is this old woman among these dead, one so old that her features have become, as it were, indistinct to my poor eyes, and I have forgotten her name. This old woman comes right up to me, amid the crowd that's harassing me, comes right up to my mouth and asks, very quietly, pulling at my skin and my swallowed lips, drawing out the folds beneath my chin, tugging at my wrinkles: "Why have you been Hartnid so little? Why have you followed the others so much, like a little puppy? Why have you always imitated the others—aped them? Like a mime in the arena. Like a reflection on the surface of water? The way a shadow pursues the advancing foot?" '

'So, this is Emmen, daughter of Emmen?'

'No, it isn't Emmen.'

'Yes, it's Emmen. Why do you lie to us? And what does Emmen say?'

'So let's say that it's Emmen, daughter of Emmen, if you insist! She's more beautiful than ever. But she's not the one asking "Why have you been Hartnid so little?" Queen Alyla reigned in that fine labyrinth of stone and boxwood that was the palace of Glendalough. But it isn't Alyla asking me the question. And it isn't Tullins beseeching me. It isn't Macra imploring. It isn't Aemilia de Gondalon at the Waters' Meeting—so young, so shy—levelling these criticisms at me. It isn't Eudocia of Byzantium on the Golden Horn that leads out towards the islet of the Naked Diver commanding me to reply. It isn't even Limni on the Plain of Limni! For me, she will always be twenty years old, but I am old, old, old! I am seventy-nine, but the two-hundred-year-old woman is saying: "They always talk of Nithard but never of you! Why have you stored up their gifts like a prostitute who hides her stash of money under the leather of her sandal? Why are you not dead when you've always lived like a dead man? Why were you Hartnid so little? Why did you pursue the kindnesses of princes like a sheep all covered in his thick, white wool, a sheep who doesn't want to miss a dandelion or a clover plant, an oat stalk or a clump of heather? Why did you close your eyes to the misdeeds of the bishops and dukes and emperors and emirs, like a man with no courage?" That's what is going on: this woman, so young and so old, so beautiful and so flabby, so blooming and so jaded, so holy and so dirty, is putting me to shame and she's right!'

Hartnid bowed his head and began to sob.

He went on: 'In some dreams, it's worse. I'm suddenly afraid she might kick away the blanket while I'm sleeping, and I'm expecting her to strike me with the flat of her hand and say, "Go away, Hartnid! There's no way I'm going to spread my thighs for you. You don't exist enough for me to feel you entering the depths of me. Truly, I find that you haven't been Hartnid enough for me to harbour the desire to take you in my arms again and hug your rough jaws to my old breasts like a man one can love and be proud of." '

'But who is this atrocious old dead woman then?'

'She's the first woman I loved. You don't know her.'

And he began to cry again.

He turned his face to the other side of the bed.

Then his loved ones began to pray for Hartnid who, as he was dying, saw again the face of the first woman for whom he'd had feelings of love.

(Among themselves, they said: 'Is it his mother?' 'No, it isn't Berehta. Bertha was always with the emperor at Aachen. She even preferred Karel to Angilbert!' 'So was it Emmen then?' 'Beyond any doubt,' said the nieces. 'They never slept together!' 'You don't need to sleep together to love each other!' argued the nieces. No one thought it could be Alyla who lived at Glendalough, nor Eudocia of Byzantium, nor Anselma of Syracuse in Sicily that faced out towards the port of Carthage, rebuilt and enhanced by the Arabs. His best friends said: 'It's Sar, it's the shaman of the Bay of the Somme. He always believed she would have married him if he could have expressed his love to her.' 'But she was a thousand years older than him!' 'No matter, she was the one he loved. There is no age in the forests. There is no poverty among tigers. There is no luxury among wolves. There is no ostentation among the wild beasts. It was with her that he was happy.')

IX

(The Book of the Poet Virgil)

1. Virgil

In *Aeneid* 6.179, Virgil wrote: One goes towards the primeval forest that was lost long ago, as soon as, imitating the insect swarms and animal packs, we grouped together to kill by preparing traps, setting up nets, piling stones on the dead, gathering armies together to kill, constituting nations that we bounded with imaginary, verbal, misty, pitiless, terrible frontiers.

In Latin: *Itur in antiquam silvam.*

The Franks went along the Rhine, along the Meuse, along the Moselle, along the Somme, along the Seine, along the Yonne, along the Loire, along the Garonne.

One goes towards the cries we heard while in the dark bellies of our mothers, up to the day when we began to stand upright and teeter towards what we interpreted as affectionate smiles and what we learnt to be beautiful faces with painted lips, which came to be like decoys beneath big hollow hairdos, above big hollow dresses, like strange, magical letters with bewitching effect.

One goes towards the birds—in music, we have strayed from them.

Itur—one goes.

Fletur—one weeps.

Where? Into that forest from before the human world, sublime vestiges of which still remain here and there, which are the finest of things,

mountain slopes,

sea shores,

sands that shift and sing the melodies of reeds and dunes,

river banks and banks of flowers—daffodils, roses, hazels, willows,

bodies that desire and bare themselves quietly in the shelter of walls or in the shade of lairs or in the artificial darkness of bedchambers, whose big solid wooden shutters they close.

Then the shutters are unlocked. The window is opened. The door is unbolted that leads out on to the heath.

You stick your head out. You take a step. You cross the threshold. You go towards the colours of the countless mosses and lichens, towards the caps of the mushrooms, each more colourful, domed and stunning than the last in the undergrowth with its thick, enchanting fragrance,

towards dawns more sparkling and dazzling than crystal, mica, jasper, gold, turquoise, opal or pearl,

and all these brilliant, marvellous, dark or reverberating shades, we have dissolved them in painting.

The tears of childhood are sufficient.

Lacrimae rerum.

The atoms that fall from the sky are the tears of things.

Thus did Virgil write that the incomparable faces and places to be found on the earth end up being tears of pain, so much do they touch the spirit like fingers, when we know we shall never see them again.

2. The Aviary of Cumae

Varro the Scholar took the trouble to explain why he had built his library, in his villa at Cumae, right alongside an enormous aviary: 'So that the souls which have left dead men's books and entered the birds should fly over their dust, find a perch and be happy.'

3. Saint John with the Eagle

Once long ago, Charles-le-Magne had wanted his daughter to learn Greek before she went to Byzantium. At that point, he had intended Princess Rothrude for Prince Constantine, son of the empress-regent Irene, who resided in the most enchanting palace in the world that looks out in contemplation upon Asia. When, at the imperial abbey of Saint-Riquier, Princess Rothrude had acquired the use of Greek from Frater Lucius, she formed the desire to translate into '*lingua romana*' the text written '*in lingua graeca*', which in the Ordinary of the Mass and in the language of the Franks now known as 'French', is called *l'Évangile de saint Jean*— the Gospel of Saint John.

Linguae cessabunt. Languages will cease. This is how, quoting the Apostle Paul, she began the translation she had resolved to make of the Prologue to John.

Once upon a time, in the beginning, the word was not. There were no men yet. All animals were beasts, and men too were beasts. The most predatory among them were not yet named, but these were already the beings called gods— that is to say, the felines and the raptors. Horses too were princes and the great stags were dukes, but they were closer to men by their beauty and the form of their sex organs. It was thus possible to intercede through them with the eagles and lions. In the absence of languages, dream images mingled with the sounds of the desires that use to their advantage the regularly shaped void which hunger and loneliness hollow out and then allow to grow within the body, to the point where it is driven mad. By dint of their reiteration, these moans wrested from them by frustration and the purrings that come from joyful satisfaction not only became lures on the lips of these beasts, but came to mumble something between their fangs, which were full of blood and lacerated sinew.

These sound-simulacra were passed on from mother to child. Speech dislodged a confusion that was barely perceived, so mingled was it with too certain feelings, with clear instances of lack, all plunged into a boundless state of alarm. But with each new birth, the moment the little living beast quitted its darkness and, slipping through the woman's narrow sex, reached the air, the light failed to absorb it entirely. Try as the light might to hold the new arrival in its brightness, in the very interior of the bedazzlement created by the rays of the sun, a nostalgia for the shadows began to be born within each. For the simple reason that breath did not exist when the body lived inside the darkness, no voice has ever been able to welcome the daylight. Hence all human beings, coming as they all did from that darkness which preceded the light, called out, as they emerged into the light, for the darkness in which they had dwelt happily, constantly sated, indistinct, invisible, fused, enfolded—replete and solid, as it were. They came from that darkness and that silence like all human beings (who had all emerged from that water where they had led an existence as solitary as it was fish-like, as fish-like as it was silent), to bear witness to the darkness, to venerate solitude, to adore silence, in order that all, in the future, should remember how the world was before there was light.

These human beings were not shadows; they came from the shadows.

The silence that surrounded them at times like a sort of aura that hovers around the clouds in a storm,

or like a sort of halo around the faces of saints,

or like a sort of golden circle around the hair of the gods,

or like a sort of cloud of light around the peaks of mountains,

had its source in that other world without light, without emptiness—that fluid, continuous world. This is why that prior silence could not move into this light-less world without perishing.

For the light does not welcome the darkness, since it illuminates it.

More than this, by sending out its brightness, light exterminates the darkness.

In the same way, those who speak never embrace the silence, because they break it.

4. Pages

Now, some of these men seemed even stranger, if that is possible, for they dissociated themselves from the group that had raised them and from the mothers who had taught them their language and tried to tame their wildness. These men persisted in silence and remained in the shadows. They were like those stones that come away from the cliff suddenly and tumble on to the beach. Silence immediately re-forms around them but it is a totally different face that they offer to view: undermined, scarred, hollowed-out, forsaken. They took themselves out of the group and retreated into the shadows that the cliff cast at its base or in its clefts.

They didn't contemplate.

They didn't sing.

They didn't speak.

They wrote on bits of bark, having first turned them over, on shards of pottery that had been broken, on driftwood, on the back of leaves when these were broad enough to take lines of letters. Even on stones, after they had spent a long time dressing them, before carving little figures on them which they barely explained to anyone. Even on bones, which they had scraped the flesh from and polished, they outlined—simplifying—the images that came from the darkness in which their dreams emerged, leaving them happily to the silence in which they had seen them. Suddenly they went into caves that were like the slit sexes of their mothers, and then with their claws of hands and with broken stones, they cut into the calcite that had covered these dark, silent vaults; they used pinewood torches that smoked beneath their eyes and made them weep as they formed their images. This 'interior of light thanks to a flame beneath their eyes' constituted what they called a 'page'. Such were the 'pages'. In lingua latina: *pagi*. In lingua romana: *pays*—settlement, village, district, country.

5. Horses

In the time of Carloman, on the banks of the Somme, the noblemen went about accompanied by their pages.

And the books were the horses.

The books could also be oxen then, pulling carts covered by stretched animal hides in which the women sheltered from the rain and the cold.

They also wrote on stags, whose skin they forgot to scrape, with the result that they remained hairy and smelly.

The hermit over there—beyond the mountain ranges of Asia, in his blue misty country—the hermit called Lao-Tzu, arriving at the Chinese border, seized by the breast the ox that was carrying him, folded it in four and slipped it into the pocket of his robe. That is how he climbed the steep steps one by one, crossed the Great Wall and went to India.

Long ago, long before the Chinese empire, long before ancient men had withdrawn into Siberia—or shut themselves away on the shifting islands of Japan—there were bisons on the cave walls.

Even before the oxen, the horses and the aurochs, there were stags with wondrous antlers.

Where does the wood in the antlers come from?

Where do the *pagi* that run beside the forests come from?

Where do the pages that open in the clearings come from?

Where do the *pays* on the shores come from?

Where does the line that the eye follows come from?

The horizon is a fiction unknown to reality.

The horizon is an imaginary line that becomes encrusted at the limit of the capacity of human sight.

On this chimerical line, the wholly linguistic soul of men writes its departures.

The hand merely follows on the page a line that exists nowhere in reality.

It is there again, all over the sky, that the birds perch and the world stops.

And why do we write with birds' feathers?

Everything is so strange on the shores of light (*in luminis oras*). A movement from left to right drives the sun itself in the eyes of its beholder. But, where the movement of that star is concerned, its dawning is on its right and that is where it is born. This is what the disciple of Saint Paul known as Saint Denis the Areopagite called the Orient. Its twilight on its left constitutes its base or, to put it another way, its retreat. This is what the Old She-wolf of the Franks refers to as the Occident of the world. And it is there one dies. The stars and the patterns that group them together appear always in the Orient, starting out from the depths of night. That is to say, they rise to the left-hand side of the person observing them. To the right of the one who has sunk to his knees and is holding out his open palms before him, on the side where the sun goes down and sets slowly in a crimson penumbra, they disappear.

This is why Isidore of Seville wrote with his right hand in 632 at Seville in the *Origins*, that the page (*pagina*) is a *pays* (*pagus*), but that the body-place that reads it is a 'black mandorla'.

6. Death in the Loire

In 849, while crossing a ford on the Loire, Walafrid the Writer, abbot of Reichenau, slipped into a trough of deep water. He was swept away like a spinning top by the swirling waters, in which he never again managed to catch his breath, and died.

7. The Sky

The 'spherical' appearance that the sky assumes at the moment when the stars come out is itself merely a fiction which our eyes invent as they raise themselves towards the revolving spasms of light.

Sar of the Somme improvised this poem:

> In the evening, every evening, something rounds
>   itself out more
> that is neither blue nor maroon nor black,
> that is like a dark circle before the night crushes it,
> like a vault or an arch that covers the water of the
>   river that passes endlessly—infinitely—
>   beneath them,
> the bats extend their delicate web beneath their
>   arms then stretch it out using their toes,
> they form something like little grey roofs flying in
>   all directions,
> the cats coming home on their velvet paws curl up
>   and slip the pads of their feet beneath the soft
>   fur covering their bellies,
> the birds, falling silent, fold their wings for the
>   night over their chubby little stomachs to
>   keep warm,
> the house roofs darken and the tiles they are made
>   of melt into each other and curve inwards,

the lawn, which runs as far as the riverbank and
    breaks off there, bulges and bends,

the bamboo stalks, ceasing to tremble, suddenly
    bow their heads,

the worm-eaten table, its wood shabby and worn,
    swells and pills like an old pair of velvet
    trousers peeling at the thigh,

the iron chairs, brown with rust, are engulfed by
    their round shadow,

the chaise longue and its fabric grow heavy and
    sunken,

the book that comes open,

the page that swells beneath the finger about
    to turn it,

me.

8. The Port of Givet

All of a sudden, in one fell swoop, I was getting into the thicker mist. I was suddenly moving more slowly in the strange frozen cottony fog. It was hard to see. I was walking very slowly through the thickets beside the water. I was coming to the Yonne barges that were standing out of the water, lifted into dry dock so that they could be repaired. At least I could make out the blurred, wet lanterns that stirred in the hazy, yellow, somewhat polluted fog.

I was going past the harbour at Givet.

I moved fearfully away from the water, listening out for the noise it made.

With my bags of books, I was advancing slowly, putting one foot cautiously in front of the other, on the slippery grey cobble stones that run along the quayside of the little harbour and are so often loosened by floods and rain.

I crossed the safer bridge more energetically, skimming my hand along the stone balustrade, though not letting it slide along it.

I passed the old Viking church where, as a child, Mallarmé went to Mass.

I was able, finally, to plant my feet in the wet grass to get to my three little houses, disturbing the pairs of mallards, taking the old towpath once again that used to lead from Sens to Saint-Julien-du-Sault and the Joigny bridge, to the city of Auxerre and the house of Cadet Rousselle, where there are no rafters and the beams exist only in dreams. I suddenly remember that dream. On the totally fogbound riverbank there were about twenty of us, men and women and small children too, right down by the water's edge. We were standing there, still and naked, waiting. The dream was a painful one. It was cold. The night was coming to an end, but it was still dark. You couldn't see clearly. In fact, it was hard to see at all.

Suddenly, it wasn't the Yonne towpath any more, but a lake in the Pyrenees near Vic, its waters quite still.

Our skin was pale and the chill gave us gooseflesh. The women's breasts and men's members hung down, unexcited. As day broke, the world grew colder. We were waiting.

The dawn spread a whiteness over the mountains, over Spain, but the sun wasn't up yet.

The earth was, at first, soft and muddy beneath our feet.

Then we were in water up to our ankles. Then the water came up to our knees. On the bank there were some tall reeds now. Also some kind of blue seaweed that got between our toes and tickled them. Suddenly our heads all turned at once. Towards the other bank, we could see a point moving far, far away on the water. A boat perhaps, but we weren't sure. If it was a boat, we couldn't make out what direction it was sailing in. We looked for unhappy, bared figures like ourselves at the other end of the world, but we couldn't see anything precise. We were getting colder and colder. We couldn't understand why the light of dawn wasn't spreading in the sky. Yet no one among us dared move. Even the four little children didn't dare move. They were cold and shivering, standing on their little legs that were sinking further and further into the silt. We were waiting.

X

(*Liber eruditorum*)

1. Li Yishan

In 834, Li Yishan devised his sordid list.

In 999, Sei Shonagon added to it.

Men shed their different skins in the evening.

Then they bring their bodies up to the smooth surface of their mirrors. They wash their faces.

They clean their fangs with little bits of wood. They wipe their claws one by one. They rub the palms of their hands to remove the dirt the day has deposited on them. They put out the light.

Naked—still phosphorescent with the light they have just extinguished—they move into the corridor, then enter the darkness of their rooms.

They open their sheets and slip into them.

They are so pale.

They are like frogs on the riverbanks that stand out against the green moss, opening wide their big, strange, bulging eyes. Our poor, first, tadpoles' world is a world of gloomy waters. Before being born and discovering the sun, we were in a place of almost total darkness, where we lived without ever breathing, like carp or crabs, squid or eels. The oldest folktales that go back to the first humans evoke that world as though it were a hell beneath the grass or a chasm in the rocks. But the Old Testament, written long ago by our Fathers in the deserts of Mount Horeb or Sinai, saw an Eden in it, where four rivers gushed forth and the first man and first woman were happy. Our body is an extraordinary vestige which the water calls to as the origin of that body or, rather, as its mother. God is endlessly inviting us to the pool of an oasis full of tree frogs and salamanders, encircled by birds. Who, when evening comes, with the door closed on the rest of the world, doesn't quiver with happiness as he slides into the hot water of a deep, scalding, scented, solitary bath? Who doesn't lie in it and close their eyes?

First of all, when the body is stripped of the clothing, the swaddling, the drawers and breeches that protect it—and sometimes embellish it—he takes care to dim the over-harsh light above the washbasin. His chest is already more at ease and his nipples stand out on renewed contact with the air. He breathes more slowly and the beating of his heart slows down. He raises a knee and, as he hoists his leg over the porcelain or cast-iron side of the bathtub, he is already beginning to relax. He dips his toes into the water where he will open himself up to the memory of his initial condition.

2. Falconry

Long ago, the King of the Franks loved to hunt with birds. The bird Charlemagne chose for his reign and also to adorn the pinnacles of his roofs and the reverse side of his coins was the eagle. The King of the Franks took over the king of the skies from the ancient kings of Rome. When an eagle flies over an army, it is an omen—the assurance of victory. In the old language used by the Franks, the lord of the eagles was called Arauz (or Arawald). The Roman emperors said, as we read in Apuleius's *Florida* CXXVI, 'When the eagle rises into the air, when it soars beyond the passing clouds, when its huge, vigorous wings have lifted it beyond the domain of rain and snow and it reaches the realm of the thunder and lightning, it gently turns, circling round from the right, using its outstretched wings as though they were the sails of a ship, and takes in at a glance the whole of the land, which it overmasters like a lord. It glides then, before swooping swiftly and silently when a sudden quarry emerges into its field of vision.'

But, mainly, the sovereign contemplates.

In the month of April 978, it came about that Otto II and his new wife Theophano, a princess from Byzantium who had landed at the port of Amalfi, wished to take the Easter sacrament at the imperial palace of Aix-la-Chapelle. They travelled there in grand style.

The King of France immediately turned crimson with rage when he learnt this.

He called on Hugh Capet and the Duke of Bourges, who gathered together an enormous army, which they immediately unleashed on to the eastern roads.

They ride night and day.

The surprise is total.

King Otto and Queen Theophano barely have time to flee from the great hall at Aachen.

The meal they have been served is still steaming on the immense rectangular table when the Frankish warriors invest the palatine villa.

The soldiers of King Hugh climb onto the roof of the old palace that Charlemagne had built and turn the bronze eagle the emperor had set facing Rome so that it faces Saxony.

At that moment, an animosity that will have no end in the history of Europe is born—in this movement of a bronze eagle that is turned towards the east in the month of April 978.

3. The Snow of Yesteryear

In the current snow that is falling in the dawn (once we see the continuous shining, sparkling mass that fills us with wonder as we emerge from sleep and open the window), the snow of yesteryear falls too.

Along with its dazzling whiteness, the current snow brings its strange, distant silence of long ago.

One opens the window and plunges into forever Time.

4. Phénu, Death

Only the old sovereign of light plays with the site, lending it its sparkle.

In the dawn, the birds await the sun.

Once daybreak lights up the riverbank and passes through the leaves on the trees, ornamenting them with openwork, the birds grow impatient to return to their companions in battle or play. The squirrel, the cat, the water snake, the sparrow and the worm.

The bee. The butterfly. The dragonfly.

But one day the dawn was made of silence.

All the animals came out on to the bank and surrounded a severed head that was spinning in the river's eddies.

Then a little blackbird, with a beak whiter than it was yellow, its feet as if caught in a lover's snare, whistled a song of indescribable beauty in the presence of the squirrel, the cat, the water snake and the swan, who all remained still.

In days gone by, they used to point out the tomb of Orpheus at the mouth of the river called the Meles,

the head sunk in the sand and barely jutting out from the particles of seashell,

the wide-open mouth still bleeding from the thyrsus blows,

still singing.

Virgil recounts that when Orpheus died at the hands of the angry Thracian women,

his thighs devoured raw without even having the hair scraped from them,

succulent and full of fat like sides of beef,

his head was lost.

It rolled down the hillside and into the river's waters,

like the head of Leander in the waters of the Bosphorus.

O mound of earth that has the colour of gold,

palluit auro,

like the head of Nithard one day long ago in the waves of the Atlantic ocean,

like the head of Butes in the—oh so blue waters—of the Tyrrhenian Sea,

the rocks surrounded it, forming the solid circle of a sombre wreath,

and the clouds gathered together above the sandy bank
and wept in the intense August heat.

5. Hartnid, Death

Sar, the shamanic poetess of the Bay of the Somme saw the
Camel get to its four feet. She answered the horse-loving
son of the pastor of Röcken with the following poem:

'The robin rejects the hard parts, then he sings!
In eggs we call these scaly parts *shells*. Farewell,
    shells!
The robin rejects even wasp wings,
he sweeps from his nest even the little sticks that
    are the legs on the bodies of grasshoppers,
then he sings.

O little bird that adores the fruits of the ivy and the
    berries of the elder!
What do you eat but the autumn,
you whose throat tends to grow red as the falling
    leaves?
You are the Autumn bird.
You are the bird of the Virginia creeper with its
    little black bells,
little balls dense and dark, like eyes looking towards
    winter,

anxious, watchful, heedful.

Your red breast is almost orange at times,

and then you're the bird of the yellow grapes that
have been allowed to wilt!

O little birds, go right ahead and get drunk on these
little golden shells!

But take care not to fall from the branch your little
claws cling to,

Or to die drowsily in air after having drunk in so
much happiness!

O you who listen to the Autumn bird,

beware of his breast as you listen to his song!

For all of us humans should prick up our ears as
soon as we hear that wondrous trill!

We should take care, even with our pleasures. We
should always mix in with them a little
abstinence and emptiness and fear!

If he sings, it is because someone among us is dying,
for the blood that rises to his breast has been
drawn from him!'

And indeed Hartnid died not long after.

6. Frater Lucius

Winter arrived all of a sudden and it was freezing cold. Old Frater Lucius was ordered by the new father abbot of the abbey dedicated to the hermit-saint Riquier to go and chop wood in the forest to heat the monks' refectory.

With his axe over his shoulder, Frater Lucius walked out of the monastery door. He went into the forest. He chose a copse of oak trees and set to work. Beneath his axe, a tree came down, then two.

Suddenly, he stops, surprised. On the low branch of an old oak a bird is singing a song so beautiful that no nightingale at night's end could compete with it. None could imitate it.

Not even a virtuosic blackbird.

Even Phenucianus, had he been there, couldn't have named it, so fulsome, developed, sublime was the melody that issued from its throat and exploded in the air.

All the other birds themselves, at the heart of the dawn, fell silent to admire it.

Even the branches of the trees fell still.

The light is strange.

The entire forest makes no sound.

Brother Lucius is standing still too. The axe has fallen from his hands. He raises his head. He remains standing there under the oak, listening to the astounding song. He is overjoyed. He is weeping. Finally, it ends.

Brother Lucius comes back at that point to the felled trees. He views them with an air of surprise. They are full of worms. Lying on the earth around them, all the leaves are dead and black. He tries to find his axe among those leaves; the handle has crumbled to dust; rust has eaten the iron; only a small round piece of the iron remains, the size of a black ear.

Brother Lucius cannot understand what has happened. Barely a moment ago he was listening to the bird.

He crouches down in the grey light.

He picks up what remains of the piece of rusty iron from his axe.

He slips the iron ear into his pocket.

He sets off towards the monastery.

When he reaches the magnificent abbey Count Angilbert had built and dedicated to the memory of Richarius the Old (or old king Riquier of the tunic woven with lilies) and its oratory of stones piled up in an arch above the *Source aux Puissances* spring, he knocks on the door.

The brother doorkeeper opens the grille but doesn't recognize him.

So Brother Lucius says again: 'I am brother Lucius'.

But the doorkeeper retorts: 'There is no brother Lucius here.'

He persists.

Then, seeing his persistence, the brother doorkeeper fetches another friar.

They look at him through the little iron window but do not recognize him.

He repeats his name and they laugh.

Little by little, the whole community of monks have gathered round the iron grille in the abbey door and are laughing.

They fetch the father abbot.

The abbot examines him in turn through the little iron door. He questions him.

Finally, unsettled by some of the answers the brother gives, the father abbot says: 'I can happily admit that you're a member of our order and you know this place you wish to enter like the back of your hand, but who is brother Lucius?'

Suddenly, one of the old monks strikes the flagstones of the courtyard with his stick.

They all turn towards him. He says he remembers having read a story set down in the monastery's daybook by an old monk who had it himself from a former friar.

Leaving Brother Lucius at the door, the friars all go up to the monastery library, following the old monk who raps the stairs with his stick. They rummage among old soot-covered vellum volumes. One of these, written on old, unscraped bear skin, tells the story of a monk called Frater Lucius who went off to cut wood in the forest and got lost. Or who had perhaps run off. Or had perhaps been eaten. They examined the dates and compared the names: it was three hundred years ago. It was in the days when Nithard was abbot, Nithard the son of Bertha and Angilbert, the grandson of Charlemagne, who was royal secretary to Charles the Bald and buried beneath the stone slab outside the old chapel's Porch of the Nativity. The monks all come back to the monastery door. They apologize to Frater Lucius whom they bring into the cloister. They salute him as their senior friar. They tell him the story they have read. Frater Lucius says, 'It seemed to me three centuries passed in little more than a quarter or half an hour.'

'A quarter or half an hour?'

'Half an hour.'

'Three hundred years?'

'Yes, three hundred years seemed to me like half an hour.'

A monk says 'That's plausible. When you listen to a song, the body stands outside of passing time.'

Another says, 'That's debatable. The body is time in person passing.'

A third friar asserts, 'Before our Christian brothers, the shamanic king Richarius and the coastal duke Angilbert colonized this piece of land, the pagan brothers, who lived here as solitaries, said, "When the soul lends an ear to the voice of a bird, it is transported into the next world".'

Frater Lucius looks at his brothers who all regard him with affection.

Very softly, Frater Lucius asks: 'You haven't by any chance seen a little black cat with a white mouth who might have come back too, have you?'

7. Lucius of Thessaly

Apuleius of Madauros said: 'Lucius tried to turn himself into an owl.'

Then Alyla of Glendalough wept: 'That was my favourite book when I was alive!'

8. The Owl

I suddenly heard a very loud noise to my right. I saw the enormous wings—a span of at least a metre—that were thrashing the grass and the earth. Then the owl flew off and clutched on to the branch of the apple tree. A soft little yellow slug was hanging from its beak. It looked worried.

'Eat, Hartnid,' I told him.

I got up from the deck chair.

I reached up on tiptoe beneath the branch. It flew down onto my fingers. It weighed perhaps fourteen ounces. I had recognized the owl. It was Hartnid.

It ate its slug on my fingers, then we spoke. We talked long into the night. When I went back into the house, it was almost dawn.

Translator's Notes

PAGE 21 | *placitum generalis*: Public judicial gathering. *Placitum* is Latin for plea.

PAGE 35 | **The Bilberry Man**: In German mythology, the *Heidelbeermann* (bilberry man) is a *Waldgeist* (a forest spirit).

PAGE 80 | **It was there that Saints . . . brought their heads to bury them . . . :** Legend has it that the martyrs carried their own heads to their place of burial, preaching sermons all the way.

PAGE 81 | **The basilica was rebuilt by Abbé Suger . . . :** Saint Dionysos or Denys gave his name to present-day Saint-Denis, north of Paris.

PAGE 106 | *Pro Deo amour . . . ne serai*: 'For the love of God and for our Christian people's and our salvation . . . If Louis keeps the oath which he swore to his brother Charles, and my Lord Charles does not keep it on his part, and if I am unable to restrain him, I shall not give him any aid against Louis nor will anyone whom I can keep from doing so.' 'Nithard's Histories' in *Carolingian Chronicles* (Bernhard Walter Scholz and Barbara Rogers trans.) (Ann Arbor, MI: University of Michigan Press, 1972), pp. 162–63.

PAGE 115 | **the black and blue jay of the oak trees**: The Eurasian jay (*garrulus glandarius*) is known in French as *le geai des chênes*.

PAGE 149 | **The *Lambeau des Mères***: Literally, the 'Mothers' Flap'. This refers to the *Plica semilunaris* or nictating membrane.

PAGE 179 | **son of the pastor of Röcken**: The reference is to Friedrich Nietzsche.